When Nightmares Come

An Investigative Wargame of Supernatural Horror

Patrick Todoroff

OSPREY GAMES
Bloomsbury Publishing Plc
Kemp House, Chawley Park, Cumnor Hill, Oxford OX2 9PH, UK
29 Earlsfort Terrace, Dublin 2, Ireland
1385 Broadway, 5th Floor, New York, NY 10018, USA
E-mail: info@ospreygames.co.uk
www.ospreygames.co.uk

OSPREY GAMES is a trademark of Osprey Publishing Ltd

First published in Great Britain in 2024

A catalog record for this book is available from the British Library.

ISBN: PB 9781472860040; eBook 9781472860057; ePDF 9781472860033;
XML 9781472860064

24 25 26 27 28   10 9 8 7 6 5 4 3 2 1

Typeset by PDQ Digital Media Solutions, Bungay, UK
Printed and bound in India by Replika Press Private Ltd.

Osprey Games supports the Woodland Trust, the UK's leading woodland
conservation charity.

To find out more about our authors and books visit www.ospreygames.co.uk.
Here you will find extracts, author interviews, details of forthcoming events and
the option to sign up for our newsletter.

Map
City of Deacon Falls map based off of a map created by iStock.com/
FrankRamspott

Contents

1 – When Nightmares Come

Tick tock, the clock strikes eleven
No moon tonight to light the heavens.

Tick tock, a midnight black
Shadows whisper at your back.
Tick tock, the clock strikes one
Now is when the nightmares come.

Brutal murders at the waterfront; missing students at University Square; antiquities stolen from the city museum; mutilated pets in a suburban community; strange creatures sighted in the state forest… sound familiar?

Always eager to bump their ratings, news feeds will dangle click-bait captions: *Bizarre! Disturbing! Mysterious!* After all, anything scandalous or sordid will hook an audience. The same goes for the eerie and the deviant.

But what if there was more to these headlines than hype? More to these crimes than the time-worn tragedy of human folly or greed? What if something *unnatural* really was going on? After all, ghost stories, fables, legends about vampires, beasts, and monsters are surprisingly *tenacious* – even after so many centuries.

Of course, modern society dismisses all that as superstition. Or, even better, makes good coin off our nagging fears by revising them into summer blockbusters.

But what if there was a kernel of truth under all that? A sharp sliver of fact buried in all that fiction? What if there really were sinister things hiding in the dark corners of the world? After all, just because we only know the distorted and diluted myths that clung so stubbornly to reach our age, it doesn't mean that those creatures didn't exist, or that they were somehow banished by science and progress. Not at all.

Perhaps they just got better at hiding.

What Is This?

When Nightmares Come (henceforth abbreviated as *Nightmares*) is a miniatures wargame of supernatural horror and occult investigation. Set in the modern era, the enemies aren't soldiers or criminals; they're unnatural creatures and inhuman beings. Things from beyond the veil, formed of malevolence and hunger. In the world of *Nightmares*, monsters are real and you're charged with hunting them down.

Nightmares is a solo/cooperative tabletop adventure wargame that uses miniature figures. Up to five players will form a team of paranormal vigilantes; self-taught occult specialists and monster hunters who call themselves the **Nightwatch**.

These self-appointed 'watchmen' have banded together to investigate mysterious disappearances, thefts, and murders, or any crime they suspect to have been committed by supernatural forces. Despite the obvious danger, not to mention the utter disbelief shown by the rest of society, these brave souls have vowed to exterminate the terrors that lurk in the shadows.

What Do I Need?

Nightmares use 288m figure and is played on a 2' x 2' game area. Players will need: figures, assorted terrain and appropriate scatter pieces, a ruler or measuring tape, a full set of polyhedral dice like those used in RPGs (two sets would be handy), a set of standard wargame blast and teardrop templates (3" and 5" diameter, plus a 8.25" teardrop), and some tokens to mark a model's status.

What Does It Involve

A typical **Case** – a full mini-campaign – can be played with thirty-six miniatures: thirty enemy models in three different types, one boss monster, and five player characters. Ideally, the enemy forces should center around a common theme (undead, vampires, were-creatures, eldritch cultists) but players are free to use which ever figures they have on hand for both monsters and hunters. A typical game – one mission with both a narrative and tactical portion – can be run in under ninety minutes.

Basic Game Mechanics

When Nightmares Come uses a range of polyhedral dice – D4, D6, D8, and D10 – to determine in-game actions, events, and resolve combat and non-combat challenges.

For player characters, three dice – D6, D8, and D10 – will define their character's core Characteristics for Narrative Scenes and form their Action Dice pool for Tactical Engagements. When attempting to act, (Move, Fight, Defend, Interact, etc.) players will roll one of those dice. A result of four or better (4+), after modifiers, is a Success. Less than four is a Failure, and players can try again with a different die type.

Occasionally, players can roll two of the same die type and choose the better result. This **Two Dice Bonus** (TDB) is given for actions related to their character specialization and simply grants players a better chance at a Success, not a chance at two Successes.

For enemy models, only one of those three die types will be their Action Die. Action Die types vary according to the quality – or **Caste** – of the enemy, and are used to resolve all their actions. Here, as well, a result of four or better (4+), after modifiers, is considered a Success. Less than four is a Failure, and enemies can try again as long as they have Action Dice remaining.

The D4 is used on certain loot or event tables and to determine enemy entry points.

Glossary of Important Terms

- **Action Dice** – D6, D8, D10. These dice represent a player character's potential to act during a Tactical Engagement.
- **Arcana** – Generic term for otherworldly matter or material with supernatural properties (think 'ectoplasmic goop'). Arcana can be collected during a Tactical Engagement and is used to upgrade weapons, items, and armor.
- **Case** – A six mission campaign. A full Nightmare.
- **Clue** – Evidence of supernatural or otherworldly activity. Found at Point of Interest locations. At least two Clues must be recovered per game to continue the Case. Extra Clues can be dispensed among NPC factions to purchase Favors.
- **Connection** – An area of the city intimately familiar to the player character. Their old neighborhood or stomping grounds, Connections are a permanent asset and used in Narrative Scenes to cancel a failed die roll in non-combat challenges.
- **Dark Spawn** – Collective term for supernatural enemies. There are three tiers or 'Castes' of Dark Spawn minions: Vermin, Horde, and Terror. The leader and final boss adversary is known as an Atrocity. (a BBEG or Big, Bad, Evil Guy/Gal).
- **Favor** – Another element of Narrative Scenes, Favors are a one-time consideration owed to a player character by a particular faction or organization in the city. Favors can be called in to cancel a failed die roll in non-combat challenges. Once 'spent', the Favor is gone. New Favors can be acquired with Clues.

- **Hunter** – (also referred to as an **Investigator**) A player character and member of the Nightwatch. There are three kinds of Hunters: combat-oriented Wardens, magic-wielding Weavers, and support specialist Wrights.
- **Incident** – A single game. Each Incident is composed of one Narrative Scene followed by a Tactical Engagement. The Narrative Scene is resolved by player discussion and group rolls. The Tactical Engagement runs for six turns.
- **Narrative Scene** – A brief fictional scenario or portion of the Case's plot that features non-combat challenges. Used to enhance the storyline and determine the disposition of the party in an impending tactical engagement.
- **Nexus** – A paranormal singularity. A local concentration of supernatural energy that draws or allows Dark Spawn to operate in that area. Contains Arcana.
- **Nightwatch** – An unofficial organization of militant vigilantes and self-taught paranormal specialists who hunt down and destroy supernatural threats to humankind.
- **Point of Interest** – (POI) One of four locations in the 2' x 2' mission area that contains Clues. Can be searched by player characters.
- **Portal** – One of four spawning points for Dark Spawn models during a Tactical Engagement. Contain Arcana.
- **Primal Attributes** – Body, Mind, Spirit. Three core elements that broadly define a player character's non-combat abilities. Used in Narrative Scenes.
- **Relic** – A unique item that focuses a Weaver's paranormal energy. Relics can be bolstered over the course of a Case to channel that energy more efficiently.
- **Satchel** – A special case or bag used by Wrights to carry their devices and elixirs. Satchels can be expanded over the course of a Case to hold more items.
- **Tactical Engagement** – A violent encounter; the tabletop wargame portion of *Nightmares*. Fangs out, literally.
- **Two Dice Bonus** – Granted for class-specific actions, players roll two of a given Action Die type and choose the better result.

What's In This Book?

This rule book is divided into nine sections: this Introduction, Character Creation, Rules of Engagement, Dark Spawn, The Supply Closet, Narrative Scenes, Tactical Engagements, Full Cases, and Last Words.

Be aware that some terms and game mechanics are mentioned early on in the book and explained in detail later. References to appropriate sections are provided wherever possible, as are examples and summaries. It's recommended that players read through this book once in its entirety, then go back to make characters before they undertake their first investigation.

Now gear up. You have monsters to kill.

Good Hunting.

2 – Character Creation

Who Are You?

Are you the sort of person who keeps a loaded shotgun and a vial of holy water by your bed? Maybe you're a quiet loner with a passable understanding of Sumerian cuneiform who scans police frequencies in their spare time? Whoever you are, you're a citizen, although not a 'normal' one, obviously.

At some point in your past, you had an encounter with the supernatural. And not in a good way – a near-death experience, a haunting, a strange dream after handling an unusual book, a séance gone very, very wrong. Whatever it was, you discovered that there are real reasons to be afraid of the dark. But, instead of pretending they didn't exist, you decided to do something about them.

Unfortunately, this makes you a bit of a fringer; someone who gets lumped in with fake moon landing theorists and flat earthers. Because, while people love to be entertained, most modern folks mock anyone who actually *believes* in ghosts, monsters, demons, and werewolves, let alone someone who insists it's their job to fight them.

This means a lot of things, not the least of which is that the odds are thoroughly stacked against you; almost everyone you confide in thinks you're crazy. The few that know you're not, worry even more for your sanity.

But more on your sanity later.

The Nightwatch: Unofficial Hunters and Investigators

Monster hunters and occult investigators have been around as long as the creatures they pursue. In other times and places, they were recognized and respected. Today, not so much. Yes, equipment has improved with technology and the tactics and techniques for tracking and killing Dark Spawn have been refined by centuries of bitter experience. In fact, the habits and vulnerabilities of all manner of unnatural adversaries have been collected and catalogued, if you know who to ask and where to look. These days, thanks to modern connectivity, that information is accessible nearly anywhere on the planet.

Despite all these advantages, one thing remains unchanged: someone has to find these creatures, confront them, and kill them. Actual people have to follow the bloody trails into lair and den, cave and coven, and put an end to the evil that festers in the darkness. There's no other way.

That's where you come in.

The Three Character Classes

While all Hunters have an unhealthy interest in the paranormal and all of them are intent on combating the things that go bump in the night, they are decidedly not in agreement on the best way to do so.

There are three classes of Hunter and, although they've been known by various names through the ages, in current terminology they are called **Wardens, Weavers,** and **Wrights**. Detailed descriptions of each class can be found below but, in broad terms, Wardens are frontline fighters, Weavers employ occult powers, and Wrights specialize in devices and potions.

Wardens prefer direct physical action. Nothing says '*Go back to the shadow*' like a fire axe and a 12-gauge shotgun. Frontline soldiers in this war, Wardens use all manner of weapons but must select either **Ranged** or **Melee** as their primary fighting method. This choice is permanent and cannot be changed. Wardens receive the Two Dice Bonus for their primary fighting method, but not the secondary.

Weavers fight fire with fire. These are, for lack of a better term, magicians. *The Lesser Key of Solomon* is bathroom reading for them. They have no problem performing exorcisms, occult rituals, or messing with dubious Victorian-era incantations to combat horrors from beyond the veil. All Weavers utilize an arcane item – called a **Relic** – to cast spells or channel supernatural power, and receive the Two Dice Bonus when doing so.

Wrights are part paranormal researcher and part specialized artificer. They insist that '*Knowledge is power.*' Whether it's an intricate clockwork device that

When playing cooperatively, it is recommended that a player control no more than 2 Hunters.

snares phantoms, an ancient Sumerian recipe to ward off demons, or hand-loaded, rune-etched ammunition, they embrace both occult lore and modern technology to engage in arcane combat. Wrights fabricate what are known as **Contraptions** and **Concoctions**, and receive the Two Dice Bonus when handling them.

Dual Modes, Dual Stat Lines

As mentioned in the previous section, each game of *Nightmares* has two facets or 'Modes' – a **Narrative Scene** and a **Tactical Engagement**. Narrative scenes are played out in a 'theater of the mind' format and resolved through player discussion and group dice roles. Tactical encounters are resolved via fast-play combat rules. All player characters have a corresponding stat line for each portion, named – you guessed it – Narrative and Tactical.

For Narrative Scenes, players assign one of three die types – a D6, a D8, and a D10 – to each of their Hunter's three **Primal Attributes: Body, Mind,** and **Spirit**. These dice will be rolled to resolve non-combat challenges in the narrative portion.

For Tactical Engagements, the three die types – D6, D8, D10 – compose what's known as the Hunter's **Action Dice Pool**. They represent that character's ability to act during a Tactical Engagement.

Full explanations of both modes are found later in this book (see pages 18 and 60). For now, understand that players will face challenges in both portions, whether that's convincing the medical examiner to grant them access to the morgue, or shooting a charging ghoul with a Glock 9mm. In either case, the base target number for success is a 4 or higher on a particular die type. These rolls are modified positively or negatively by things like circumstances, equipment, and terrain.

Narrative Stat Basics

Narrative Scenes are a light, role-playing element of *Nightmares*. A Narrative Scene's obstacles and opportunities are spelled out in the location brief and, while often tense or difficult, are always non-combat challenges.

Here is where the character's **Primal Attributes** – their **Body, Mind,** and **Spirit** – come into play. These narrative interludes, or 'cutscenes', give all the Hunters a chance to perform tasks like persuasion, research, investigation, and stealthy infiltration. General challenges are included in the location briefs but the specifics of those narrative portions are left to the group's imagination. Simply know that success or failure in these scenes determine a party's relative advantages or disadvantages for the imminent confrontation with supernatural horrors.

Primal Attributes

The three die types – D6, D8, and D10 – are used to define a Hunter's physical prowess, intellectual capacity, and underlying strength of character. Assign one die type to each of these core characteristics, or **Primal Attributes**. One die type to their Body, one to their Mind, and one to their Spirit. One die type for each Primal Attribute. Any social, mental, spiritual, or physical non-combat challenge in a Narrative Scene is resolved by rolling the appropriate Primal Attribute die.

Example 1: Terrence Locke – Warden

Terry is an 'in-your-ugly-face' monster hunter. He's strong and brave, but wasn't exactly at the top of the class (there are moments you'd swear that the wheel is turning but the hamster is dead). While he isn't the guy to bypass a warehouse alarm, he's more than ready to go toe-to-toe with a ghast.

Terrence Locke – Warden		
Body	**Mind**	**Spirit**
D10	D6	D8

Example 2: Sister Margaret – Weaver

Sister Margaret wields a vicious ruler against cheating students. She can browbeat the city clerk at Records and Zoning. And she calls on divine power when facing demons from the infernal plane. Just don't expect her to run after a fleeing cultist.

Sister Margaret – Weaver		
Body	**Mind**	**Spirit**
D6	D8	D10

Example 3: Anton Chemia – Wright

Anton is a machinist who goes for a jog along the river every morning before spending the rest of the day at his workbench. Shy, meticulous, and with an encyclopedic knowledge of the city subway system going back nearly a century, he's the quiet type who avoids confrontation when he can. He is particularly skittish when it comes to things with fangs or claws, and leathery wings are definitely out.

Anton Chemia – Wright		
Body	**Mind**	**Spirit**
D8	D10	D6

Tactical Stat Basics

Tactical Engagements are where the majority of game time is spent in *Nightmares* (this is a miniature wargame, after all).

Although there are occasions for non-violent interaction with NPCs and certain terrain items during a Tactical Engagement, for the most part, combat missions are potentially fatal encounters with hostile supernatural creatures.

In a Tactical Engagement, each player character has an Action Dice Pool composed of one D6, one D8, and one D10 to represent their potential to fight, search for clues and valuable materials, and keep moving during their turn.

Regardless of their class, Terry, Sister Margaret, and Anton each have all three die types available during Tactical Engagements. Also, they receive different benefits for actions related to their specific character class. However, certain physical capabilities – their in-game, tabletop stats – are derived from their Primal Attributes. This is what makes them different from one another during play.

Derived Stats

Although Narrative Scenes and Tactical Engagements are distinct modes of the game, and the different stat lines are referenced during their relevant portion, they are interlinked. The Primal Attribute values not only generate an overall picture of a character's constitution, cognition, and courage, but they also impact their capabilities in Tactical Engagements. This makes a simple but effective way to create personalities with unique features that also meshes with the game's character class tropes. Specifically, a Hunter's **Move Rate**, number of **Equipment Slots, Extraction Efficiency,** and **Resolve** are all derived from the Primal Attribute die types. **Relic**

Charge and **Satchel Capacity** for Weavers and Wrights are also dependent on Primal Attributes, but that is only relevant to those character classes.

Derived Stat Table		
Derived Stat	**Linked Primal Attribute**	**Formula**
Move Rate	Body	1/2 die value in inches.
Equipment Slots	Body	1/2 die value for number of Mundane items.
Extraction Efficiency	Mind	1/2 die value in usable Arcana gathered per salvage action
Resolve	Spirit	1/2 die value in number of Hits per turn before a Dread roll is required
Relic Charge *Weaver Only*	Spirit	1/2 die value. Relic's starting spell charge capacity. The number and power of Spells available during a single game.
Satchel Capacity *Wright Only*	Mind	1/2 die value. Satchel's starting carry capacity for Contraptions and Concoctions.

Example 1: Terrence Locke – Warden

Terrence Locke – Warden		
Body	**Mind**	**Spirit**
D10	D6	D8

Referencing the table above, Terry, our beast-slaying Warden, would have:

- A Move Rate of 5" per action (1/2 of Body D10).
- He'd be able to carry five items (5 Equipment Slots from 1/2 of Body D10).
- He can extract only three units of Arcana any time he scrounges from a supernatural node, such as a Portal or Nexus (1/2 of Mind D6).
- He would be able to endure four Hits before he needed to roll against Dread (1/2 of Spirit D8).
- Relic Charge and Satchel Capacity do not apply as he's neither a Weaver nor a Wright.

Example 2: Sister Margaret – Weaver

Sister Margaret – Weaver		
Body	**Mind**	**Spirit**
D6	D8	D10

On the other hand, Sister Margaret skipped gym to go to the library:

- Her Move Rate is 3" per action (1/2 of Body D6).
- She can carry three items (3 Equipment Slots from 1/2 of Body D6).
- She does know how to extract a bit more Arcana – four units per Portal or Nexus (1/2 of Mind D8).
- She can take five Hits before existential Dread threatens to overwhelm her (1/2 of Spirit D10).
- As a Weaver, she can channel five Spells (prayers, surges of supernatural energy) through her Relic each Tactical Engagement (1/2 of Spirit D10). This number can be increased over the course of a Case by spending Arcana.
- Satchel Capacity does not apply.

Example 3: Anton Chemia – Wright

Anton Chemia – Wright		
Body	**Mind**	**Spirit**
D8	D10	D6

Although timid, Anton considers himself the brains of the team:

- His Move Rate is 4" per action (1/2 of Body D8).
- He can carry four items (4 Equipment slots from 1/2 of Body D8)
- He is an expert at extracting Arcana – five units per Portal or Nexus (1/2 Mind D10).
- His logical, orderly mind is easily unsettled, Anton can only take three Hits a turn before starting to panic (1/2 Spirit D6).
- He is not a Weaver, so Relic Charges do not apply.
- As a Wright, his Satchel can hold five specialized items (1/2 of Mind D10). This number can be increased over the course of a Case by spending Arcana.

Equipment Slots versus Recovered Items

Equipment Slots represent carried gear and items that are readily accessible during a Tactical Engagement. Recovered objects, such as Clues and Arcana – as well as any similar elements specific to the player's own narrative – are automatically put in the Hunter's cargo pockets, backpack, messenger bag, fanny pack, etc. These are bottomless and there is no limit on the number of such things a Hunter can carry.

Character Class Advantages

Although every player's Hunter receives the same Action Dice Pool in Tactical Engagements, they receive an advantage when attempting an action related to their class. Known as the 'Two Dice Bonus' or 'rolling with advantage', this benefit applies only to Tactical Engagements.

In the following instances, players may roll two of their selected action die type and choose the better result:

- **Wardens** receive the Two Dice Bonus when attacking with their primary fighting method, either Ranged or Melee.
- **Weavers** receive the Two Dice Bonus when channeling supernatural power through their Relics (i.e. casting Spells).
- **Wrights** receive the Two Dice Bonus when employing occult instruments and applying special potions – their Contraptions and Concoctions.

Character Abilities

In *Nightmares*, basic Abilities are available to all character classes. Used in Tactical Engagements they represent inherent strengths or aptitudes. Note that, although there are only four to choose from, they are package deals, with related benefits bundled together. Players may select one, and only one, per Hunter. This choice is permanent for as long as that Hunter remains alive.

Abilities List

1. **Fast on their Feet:** The Hunter gets +1" to Movement rate and no penalty for crossing obstacles, climbing, jumping, or falling from any height.
2. **Stone-Cold, Cast-Iron Bad-Ass:** The Hunter gets a +2 bonus to all Terror and Dread rolls.

3. **Pack Rat:** The Hunter has one additional Equipment slot and can re-roll one die on any failed Interact rolls at a Point of Interest, Portal, or Nexus for free. Players must abide by the result of the second roll.
4. **Slippery and Sneaky:** Any rolls to disengage from Melee have a +2 bonus and the Hunter always receives an additional +1 modifier to their Dodge Defend rolls when in Cover.

Character Class Skills

Class Skills differ from Abilities in that they are learned fields of expertise related to a specific character class. Hunters start with one Skill and can only choose from the Skills that are available to their class. Hunters may acquire a second Skill over the course of a Case by earning and spending Advances (see page 75).

Warden Skills

- **Marksman/Blunt Trauma:** An expert at inflicting damage with either a two-hand Ranged or two-hand Melee weapon (Heavy or Awkward Heft). All Dark Spawn must subtract 1 from their Dodge Defend rolls. This benefit only pertains to the Warden's primary fighting method and is in addition to any other damage modifiers from a particular weapon or circumstance.
- **Dual Wield:** Armed with two, one-hand weapons (Light Heft), the Hunter may attack a single adversary with both weapons as one action. The weapons must be of the same type, either one-hand Ranged or one-hand Melee. The first die type for the attack is the player's choice. The second is a D6. This D6 action dice is free only for these attacks and is not part of the player's Action Dice Pool (i.e. it does not use a player's D6 Action Die). Warden class Hunters may apply the Two Dice Bonus and roll two of each die type and select the better result of each pair. In the example presented, the Warden with twin Glocks would roll 2D8 and 2D6, then choose the better result of each D6/D8 pair.
- **Bar Brawler:** 'Outnumbered' penalties do not apply when this character is in melee with multiple opponents, and they always add one to their melee attack rolls.

Example: A Dual Wield Hunter fires two pistols at a werewolf. They select their D8 and receive a free D6. If both attack rolls succeed, then the werewolf must defend against two Hits.

Weaver Skills

- **Weirdly Prescient:** Hyper-sensitive to paranormal emanations? Or perhaps excessive pharmaceutical recreation during their teenage years? Regardless of the reason, this Hunter's 'doors of perception' were flung wide open. This character gets a free D6 roll at the start of the Adversary phase after the Dark Spawn appear at the portals but <u>before they take any action</u>. If the Weaver's D6 roll is successful (4+) they may immediately take a free Move action.
- **Arcane Dominion:** Intensive study of arcane energy allows this character to automatically succeed when closing a Portal or Nexus. Base-to-base contact with the Portal or Nexus is required and an Action die must be given up or 'spent', but no 4+ roll is required.
- **Magical Mulligan:** Divine favor? Remarkable powers of concentration? Whatever it is, the Hunter has an innate affinity for occult power. At the start of a Tactical Encounter, the Weaver rolls a D4 and notes the result. The Weaver may reroll half that number (rounded up) of failed or fumbled spellcasting rolls that mission. They must abide by the results of the second roll.

Wright Skills

- **Efficient Extraction:** Arcane affinity combined with meticulous research of Dark Spawn physiology means the Hunter automatically receives one unit of Arcana whenever they kill a Dark Spawn adversary. Also, they receive half 1D4 Arcana (rounded up) in addition to their Extraction Efficiency when pulling Arcana from a Portal or Nexus.
- **No Shit, Sherlock:** intense scrutiny and a suspicious nature mean this Hunter can find two Clues when searching a Point of Interest location rather than one. However, they must expend another Action to search the POI a second time.
- **Home-Brewer:** This Hunter's potions and grenades are extremely potent, at least, most of the time. Roll a D6 whenever they apply a Concoction or use a Contraption. This roll is free. On a 5+, the effects are twice as a powerful (e.g. two wounds healed, double damage modifier, extra movement boost). On a 2–4, the effects are standard. On a 1, the potion or grenade is a dud and has no effect.

Character Creation Summary

There are **ten** steps to create a Hunter for *Nightmares*:

1. Select Character Class – either a Warden, Weaver, or Wright.
2. Assign die types to the Hunter's three Primal Attributes as preferred, usually to optimize their Character Class capabilities. D6, D8, and D10 to Body, Mind, and Spirit.
3. Determine the Hunter's derived stats: Movement and Equipment Slots from their Body; Extraction Efficiency from their Mind; Resolve from their Spirit.
4. Select a General Ability
5. Select a class-specific Skill
6. Note the Hunter's Action Dice Pool and class-related Two Dice Bonus.
7. Assign the Hunter's Weapons and Protection, making note of Range, Firepower, and Frequency. Make note of any class-related restrictions. See Section 5 for details.
8. Select equipment and items for the Hunter's available Equipment Slots. See Section 5 for details.
9. If a Warden, choose their Primary Fighting Style: Ranged or Melee. If Weaver, determine their initial Relic Charge (derived from Spirit die type). If Wright calculate their initial Satchel Capacity (derived from Mind die type).
10. For the Narrative Scenes, select the character's Connection and determine their two starting Favors. See Sections 6 and 8.

The WYSIWYG – IDM Ethos

'**What you see is what you get. Important details matter**' simply means models should have the weapons and armor stated on their character sheet. I don't mean counting rivets or arguing over Kevlar or ceramic inserts. There's no need to swap out weapon accessories between missions or purchase the same miniature in multiple poses/stances.

Important Details Matter. That said, if you stat out a Weaver with a shotgun, make sure it has one. Dual-wielding Warden? Find a mini with two weapons. The intention is to help players identify their models and capabilities quickly, eliminate confusion, and smooth play. It's meant to deter abuse rather than be a straitjacket or a source of tension.

EXAMPLE CHARACTER

Terrance Locke				
Character Class: Warden	Primary Fighting Method: Melee			
Primal Attribute	Body: D10	Mind: D6		Spirit: D8
Move Rate – *Distance in inches per Move action*	5"			
Equipment Slots – *Number of items he can carry*	5			
Extraction Efficiency – *Amount of arcane material he can recover from a Portal or Nexus*		3		
Resolve – *The number of Hits/turn he can take before he must roll for Dread*				4
Relic Charge/Satchel Capacity	NA			
Action Die Pool				
Free Move + 1D6, 1D8, 1D10				
Two Dice Bonus				
Attack rolls in Melee (roll two of the same die type and choose better result				
General Ability				
Slippery and Sneaky – Any rolls to disengage from Melee have a +2 bonus and the character always receives an additional +1 modifier to their Dodge Defend rolls when in Cover.				
Class Skill				
Bar Brawler – Outnumbered penalties do not apply when this character is in melee with multiple opponents and they always add +1 to their melee attack rolls.				
Connections				
Waterfront (See Section 6, page 61, for details)				
Favors				
Pick any two NPC factions (See Section 6, page 61, for details)				

Weapons and Equipment					
Weapon	**Heft**	**Uses/Turn**	**Range**	**Rate of Fire**	**Damage**
Glock 17	Light, one-hand	3	1"- 12"	1	1
Tonfa	Light, one-hand	Unlimited	Melee	1	1
Equipment Slots					
Glock	Tonfa	First Aid Kit	First Aid Kit	Kaiju Energy Drink	

3 – Rules of Engagement

Underneath the horror and supernatural warfare theme, *Nightmares* is a straightforward tabletop wargame that uses four types of polyhedral dice – the D4, D6, D8, and D10 – to determine the outcome of game challenges and resolve combat. The D4 is used for most random location challenges, such as the entry points for Dark Spawn adversaries. The D6, D8, and D10 are used to determine the success or failure of a model's actions. An extra D6 can come in handy for tracking game turns.

Turn Sequence

Nightmares uses the simple 'IGO-UGO' turn sequence during Tactical Engagements. This means that the Hunters will activate all their miniatures, one at a time, and resolve all their Actions. Once that's complete, the Dark Spawn models will activate and do the same. Once all models on both sides have gone, the turn ends.

Models can be activated in any order, but each model must complete its activation before another can go. If players are determined to fight among themselves, they can roll a die to determine who activates in what order.

Hunters First

Hunters always activate first in a Tactical Engagement. Turns and activations continue back and forth in that order until the Hunters achieve their objectives, retreat off board, or the turn limit is reached. Once activated, a model must finish all its actions before another can go.

Turn Limit

Between skeptical law enforcement, nervous neighbors, creepy noises, bestial roars, and the sound of gunfire, a single Tactical Engagement on a 2' x 2' area is limited to six turns. That means the player characters have to move fast and stay focused if they want to gather clues and any recover valuable Arcana to aid them in their investigation.

- Exception: Any Nightwatch team brave or crazy enough to restrict themselves solely to melee and non-gunpowder ranged weapons (no grenades, flame throwers or chem-sprayers, etc.) may remain at the scene for a seventh, extra turn. Player characters must exit the area by the end of the final turn, but any remaining Portals will not spawn new adversaries.

Action Dice

For the Hunters, three dice – a D6, D8, and D10 – constitute their **Action Dice Pool**. Those die types are used whenever a Hunter's model is activated and attempts in-game actions during the Tactical Engagement phase of an Incident. Action Dice can be used in any order, but each type can only be used once. The Action Dice Pool is renewed every turn.

Dark Spawn adversaries use the same die types – known as their **Caste Die** – in a slightly different manner. Each caste rolls one specific die type – and only that type – when attempting actions and resolving combat (see Section 4, page 36, for more on Dark Spawn).

Actions and Successes – Player Characters

When activated, each player character has the potential to perform up to three Actions during their game turn, in addition to a Free Move. A successful Action is achieved by rolling a 4+ (plus or minus modifiers) on a D6, D8, or D10 Action Die. A roll of less than 4 (after modifiers) is considered a failure and the player can try an action again using a different die type – so long as they have dice remaining in their Action Dice Pool.

To act, simply declare the intended Action (Move, Shoot, Interact, etc.), select one of the die types in the Dice Pool, and try for a 4+, accounting for modifiers and penalties. Bear in mind that any given model must fully finish its activation before another model can activate.

Diminishing Possibilities

To represent the stress and diminishing possibility of accomplishing tasks in a tense combat situation, each die type can only be used once. One chance with a D10, one with a D8, and one with a D6. That's it. Although special circumstances permit Hunters to roll two of a given die type at times, each Die Type can only be used once per a model's activation.

In either case, once the character's Action Dice Pool is depleted, they can no longer act that game turn. This means that players must prioritize their intended actions and allocate whichever Die Type they feel gives them the best chance at success. Remember, die types do not have to be used in any particular order.

Free Move

All models in *Nightmares* receive one 'Free Move' per activation. This is in addition to their action dice pool and allows them to move up to their full Move Rate without expending an Action Die. Also note that some Hunters may forego their Free Move to perform certain other actions instead, such as reload a weapon, apply first-aid to themselves, or imbibe a concoction. Dark Spawn do not have this option and can only use their Free Move to move.

Two Dice Bonus

A majority of action rolls are attempted with a single die. However, Character Class specializations offer a better chance at succeeding at certain actions. In those cases, the Hunter can roll two dice of a particular type and use the best result. This is called the **Two Dice Bonus.**

In *Nightmares*, this **Two Dice Bonus** applies to specific in-game actions related to a Hunter's field of expertise. Keep in mind that the Two Dice Bonus does not give a player an opportunity for two successes, merely two chances to succeed at a given task.

Critical Successes and Critical Fails

Whenever a Hunter naturally rolls the highest value on an action die type, (a 6 on a D6, 8 on a D8, etc) it is considered a **Critical Success** and they receive a minor benefit related to that particular action.

If the action was an Attack, the damage of their weapon is increased by 1. If they were Moving, they receive an additional 1" to their Move Action. If the Action was an Interact of any sort, the model receives an immediate extra D6 action. Critical Successes do NOT apply to Dodge Defend rolls, as the body armor/protective gear is doing most of the heavy lifting there.

For Two Dice Bonus-related actions, the chance of success is already boosted, so in those instances, **both dice** must show the highest value. If so, the benefit is increased by one more level: +2 to weapon Damage, 2" to Movement, an extra D8 action. Otherwise, those actions are simply a standard success.

Critical Fails occur only when a Two Dice Bonus roll results in double ones. In this case, the action fails and the character's activation ends immediately.

Dark Spawn adversaries **do not get** Critical benefits or penalties.

Die rolls resulting from Critical Successes do not yield additional critical results.

Actions

Fighting supernatural enemies is hard, dirty work. Below is a list of actions that can be performed during a model's activation.

Aim – (Melee or Ranged)

The term 'Aim' is used here in the sense of taking a moment to find an adversary's vulnerability. If in Melee, it's seeing an opening in their armor or an opportunity to strike. If performed before a ranged attack, that's zeroing in on a particular spot or exposed portion. A successful Aim Action means the vulnerability/opportunity was identified. A failure means the effort was spent but frustrated. Successful or not, an Aim action must always be followed by an appropriate Attack action. A successful Aim action grants a +1 bonus to the attacker's Attack roll as well as a -2 penalty to the target's Dodge Defend roll.

Attack (Melee)

Attack an enemy model while in base-to-base contact. Unless a special Skill, weapon, or Trait specifically dictates otherwise, one Action grants one Attack.

Attack (Ranged)

Attack an enemy model with a ranged weapon. The enemy model must be within the weapon's stated effective range and Line of Sight of the attacking model. Unless a special Skill, weapon, or Trait specifically dictates otherwise, one Action grants one Attack.

Concentrate Fire

Hunters only. This special combat action can be initiated by any Hunter but only with the express cooperation of all other Hunters involved.

Concentrate Fire allows multiple Hunters to perform a combined ranged attack on a single target. If the following conditions are met, this special action provides bonus modifiers to the Ranged Attack roll as well as a penalty to the target's Dodge Defend roll. The modifiers are equal to the number of participants.

Concentrate Fire Conditions

1. Concentrate Fire order is a special action performed by the initiating character that requires a 4+ success roll (after modifiers) on any action die type.
2. All attackers involved must have Line of Sight and Range to the target.
3. All attackers must be within 8" of the initiating model.
4. All attackers must have an action die to spend.

When performing **Concentrate Fire**, the initiating model is the central point of reference. It is done during that Hunter's activation and their Action Die is used for the Ranged Attack roll. The Two Dice Bonus is permitted where applicable, as is any special rule from another Skill or Weapon that initiating model has or is equipped with. Any other Skills or weapon advantages from other attackers are abstracted, being rolled into the combined attack for this special action.

Concentrate Fire Process

Clearly declare the Concentrate Fire action then specify the attackers and target model. The initiator must then roll a 4+ on any Action Die type to rally the group and focus their attention. Concentrate Fire is a distinct action, separate from a Ranged Attack. A failed roll means the effort was spent but frustrated.

Following a successful call to concentrate fire, all participating models must spend one action die from their Action Die Pool for that turn. Yes, it can be their lowest type. Yes, this is a pre-emptive, partial activation for the secondary shooters involved.

Once that is done, a single Ranged Attack roll is made by the initiating model using a die from their Action Dice Pool. Again, this can be any remaining die type, and any Two Dice Bonus, Skills, or weapon advantages possessed by the initiating model are applied to this roll.

This Ranged Attack roll is modified by +x, where x = total number of attackers involved. If the attack roll is successful, the target's Dodge Defend roll is then also penalized by -x. Remember to account for any Cover and obstructions.

So, shoot the Dark Spawn with a dice roll +x. If it's a Hit, the target rolls Dodge Defend with a dice roll -x.

Concentrate Fire Example

Terry Locke (Warden) has lured a hulking, sewer-dwelling Ghoul (D10, Terror Caste adversary) into an ambush in an alley between Booker's Pawn Shop and the Golden Banana Gentlemen's Club. He calls on two fellow Hunters to help and uses his D6 Action Die to initiate Concentrate Fire. He rolls is a 5. He can proceed.

His fellow hunters must now each donate an Action Die from their pool. Then Terrance rolls his D10 for a Ranged Attack. His Attack roll is modified by +3 (the total number of attackers involved) and the Ghoul's D10 Dodge Defend roll is penalized by -3.

As a Warden, Terrance rolls 2D10 and selects the better result because he assigned his Two Dice Bonus to Ranged Attack Primary Fighting Style.

A sharp burst of gunfire and the slavering Ghoul topples in several pieces. Terrance then uses his remaining D8 to Move and take up a better position on a nearby Portal.

Dodge Defend

Simply put, this is an attempt to avoid injury. The target number for a Hunter's Dodge Defend roll is related to their Armor, and subject to any pertinent Cover or Equipment modifiers. Dark Spawn minions use their caste Quality Die type. An Atrocity references their Armor.

Interact

A catch-all action referring to most non-combat interaction with other models and special scenic elements. This Action covers things like applying a First-Aid kit to an ally, searching a Point of Interest Location for clues, shutting down a Portal or Nexus, or opening a jammed door. An Interact Action is a simple task that requires a block of time, effort, and base-to-base contact with the particular item.

Move

Moving your model up to its maximum Move Rate. Movement does not have to be in a straight line and the model need not move the full distance. Terrain modifiers may affect movement.

Overwatch

Hunters and Atrocities only. Overwatch is simply reserving actions in order to interrupt your opponent. The player must set aside two action dice in order to use one for a single action during an enemy model's activation. To break Overwatch, the player declares when the action will be attempted and what that action is. For example, 'As soon as that werewolf comes out from behind the cemetery wall, I'm shooting'. Then both reserved dice are rolled and the player selects the better result.

If a Hunter interrupts an enemy with a Two Dice Bonus action, such as a melee-oriented Warden swinging their cricket bat, they roll both reserved dice and may reroll one failed die if necessary.

Reload

Specific to reloading a single shot weapon. For single-shot weapons, it is presumed the Hunter carries enough ammunition on their person for an entire battle. A Hunter may spend their Free Move to Reload their own weapon, otherwise it requires a successful personal Use or Interact Action.

Special/Skill Check

Special or Skill Check Actions are complex tasks associated with mission objectives or a game's narrative during a Tactical Engagement (Narrative Scenes follow different rules). These tasks usually require several steps and have some degree of difficulty. The steps are performed through multiple actions and the difficulty is expressed by a negative modifier to the Action Dice rolls.

For example, untying a hapless victim from a makeshift sacrificial alter might take one action at difficulty penalty of -1. Pouring gasoline on a clutch of giant spider eggs may take two actions at difficulty of -2. Knocking down a totem carved with writhing demonic sigils would take three actions with a -3 penalty.

Complex tasks like this usually require a model to be in base-to-base contact with a particular terrain item. Specific action cost and difficulty for Special Actions varies from task to task and mission to mission. Successes can be tracked by tokens near the terrain item or on a Hunter's stat sheet. Failures mean the action was spent in frustration but they do not undo any previous success.

Unless specified by the scenario, successes on special actions and complex tasks can be 'banked', meaning they do not have to be accomplished without interruption or performed by the same person. However, special Skills or gear may give a particular Hunter an advantage on certain tasks.

Throw Grenade/Weapon

Use the same process as for making a Ranged Attack. Some thrown weapons, hand grenades and the like, use the Indirect Ranged Attack rules (see page 28).

Use

Another catch-all action for Hunters, it refers to personal actions, such as imbibing an Energy Drink or Potion, Reloading, or applying a First Aid kit to themselves, or any other minor action involving only the Hunter. In general, these kinds of actions can be taken in lieu of the character's Free Move once per activation, otherwise they require an Action Die roll to perform.

Movement

A Hunter's base Move Rate is derived from their Body Primal Attribute (half the die value in inches). Dark Spawn have a suggested default move rate of 6". This can be modified by Dark Spawn Traits and player preference.

Models do not have to move in a straight line and they do not have to move the full distance. All Movement measurements start from the **front** of the model's base and end at the **rear** of the model's base. This does add an additional base width to the movement. It also cuts down on arguments.

Climbing, Difficult Terrain, Obstacles, Jumping, and Falling

Climbing ladders or using stairs is done at standard Movement rate. A Hunter can also scale tall vertical surfaces at a rate of half their standard Move Rate. A Hunter with a 5" Move Rate could scale 2.5" in one Move Action. While a Hunter is attempting to scale a tall structure, such as the exterior of a building, they can only take Move Actions until they have finished climbing (clinging like a scared cat to the sheer surface between activations). No other action is possible until they are back on a level surface.

Difficult Terrain is any level ground that hinders normal movement, such as a stretch of rubble, an oily patch, a swamp, a slimy sewer floor, or any similar location determined by the scenario. Crossing a section of difficult terrain is done at half speed, so a 2" patch of swamp would require a 4" move.

Obstacles are similar to Difficult Terrain. An Obstacle is any low scenery item, such as a wall less than 1" high, a stack of crates, or an open window. Unless a Hunter has a special ability, moving over or through Obstacles requires minor additional effort and is done at the cost of an additional 1" of movement per obstacle. Therefore, a model moving 2" then hopping over a low wall would spend 3" to end up immediately on the other side of that wall.

Jumping narrow spans up to 1" wide on the same level incurs a cost of an additional 1" of movement, similar to traversing Obstacles. Jumping distances greater than 1" is not allowed without special abilities or equipment.

Remember that every model receives one Free Move per Turn. This Free Move is not part of the model's three Actions/ Action Dice Pool. The Free Move can be taken any time during the model's activation and can be used for non-standard movement such as climbing, jumping, and crossing obstacles or difficult terrain." However, Free Movement cannot be split between different actions and any further movement must be attempted with a roll from the Action Dice Pool.

Any Prone model (falling, a blast, or similar effect) should be laid on its side. Prone Hunters suffer a -2 penalty to their Dodge Defend rolls while down. Dark Spawn suffer a -4. Prone models must expend an Action to get back up on their feet and cannot perform any other Action until they do so.

Any model that **falls** off a high surface must make a Dodge Defend roll at a -1 penalty for every story fallen. At 28mm scale, every 2" height counts as a story. Even if a model avoids damage from falling, they are considered Prone when they land.

Terrain

Terrain in *Nightmares* serves three purposes. The first is aesthetic; crowded alleys and side streets, the city cemetery, the antiquities wing of a museum, wherever your scenario takes place, there are few things quite as cool as a well-dressed game table. The second is to block and or alter a model's Line of Sight and movement ability. The third purpose is to serve as protection once the combat starts.

There are three types of protective terrain: **Obstructions, Concealment, and Cover.**

Obstructions are low, intervening scenic items that obscure but do not completely block the attacker's Line of Sight. These scenic items and scatter terrain pieces are less than the height of a human model and come into play when neither attacker nor defender is in base-to-base contact with it – the piece simply interrupts a direct-fire Ranged Attack. We're talking about shooting over things like a guard rail, a (very) low stone wall, or pile of rubble. The hardness or density of the item is irrelevant; if the defender is not in base-to-base contact with it relative to the angle of attack, the scenic item counts as an Obstruction.

Concealment is a scenic item representing low density material like plant undergrowth, a pile of trash bags, or even a split rail fence. These things hide rather than protect. In this case, a defending model must be in base-to-base contact with the terrain item relative to the angle of attack in order to receive any benefit.

Cover is protection. Timber, stone, concrete barriers, or any other hard material that can stop or deflect an attack. Again, the defending model must be in base-to-base contact with the terrain item relative to the angle of attack in order to receive any protective benefit.

Terrain Modifiers are expressed as penalties subtracted from the attacker's roll. Cover grants a bonus to a Defender's Dodge Defend roll. Apply common sense and fair play in terrain disputes, imagining how the combatant represented by a model would make the best use of cover and concealment. Grazing the base or touching a small portion of the static pose miniature does not make it a viable target (here's your excuse to buy a cool laser pointer).

Terrain Modifiers
- **Obstruction**: -1 to Attack Roll. Cumulative with other Obstructions, Concealment, and Cover.
- **Concealment**: -2 to Attack Roll.
- **Cover**: -2 to Attack Roll and + 2 to Dodge Defend Roll.

Combat

Nightmares is a tabletop wargame about fighting monsters, so this section is very much at its heart. Be sure to read this portion thoroughly before setting up to play.

Combat: The Short Version

Whether it's a ranged attack with a hunting rifle or an 'in-your-partially decomposed-face' smack with a cricket bat, to Attack a foe, an appropriately armed Hunter selects one die type from their Action Dice Pool, designates the target, and rolls, hoping for a success on a 4+ (+/- modifiers). Two Dice Bonus benefits apply to relevant Skills and Actions, and multiple Attacks can be made in a single activation, so long as the activated model has Action Dice remaining in their Action Dice Pool.

When Dark Spawn adversaries Attack, they select one of their caste-level dice and do the same. Dark Spawn may have Traits that give them specific advantages on Attacks, but they do not receive a Two Dice Bonus (see pages 35 for Dark Spawn).

Dodge Defend Roll

If an Attack roll was a success and the target was hit by either a Melee or Ranged Attack, the defender must then make a Dodge Defend roll.

A 4+ (+/- modifiers) means the Attack's damage was avoided or deflected. A result of less than 4 (+/- modifiers) means the defender receives a Wound.

Dodge Defend Die Types

For Hunters, their Dodge Defend die type is related to their Armor. This is usually a D6 (See The Supply Closet for details, page 44). Dodge Defend rolls can be modified by Cover, weapon upgrades, and similar. However, when the fangs are out and unnatural energies are swirling in the cold, night air, your average Hunter in relatively inconspicuous protective clothing stands a roughly 50/50 chance of avoiding damage.

Note that this different from Dark Spawn adversaries. They use their Caste die type when rolling to defend. The exception is the Atrocity, who is more of an enhanced character, similar to the Hunters.

Melee Combat – The Long Version

Melee combat can only occur when models are in base-to-base contact. The only exception is when combatants are on opposite sides *and* in base-to-base contact with an Obstacle, such as a short hedge or wall (terrain roughly half the height of a regular human model). In this specific instance, terrain modifiers are negated and every attack by both parties is subject to a -2 penalty to their Attack rolls. Dodge Defend rolls are calculated normally without Cover modifiers.

When two models are in Melee combat, the attacking model – the active side – selects a die type and rolls to attack, with a success on a 4+ (+/- modifiers). Each success counts as one Hit. The Two Dice Bonus applies to melee-oriented Wardens.

For every Hit suffered, the Defender then makes a Dodge Defend Roll on their appropriate die type, with a success on a 4+ (+/- modifiers). Each Dodge Defend roll success means one Hit was blocked or deflected. Any unsuccessful Dodge Defend rolls result in a Wound. Unless specified otherwise, all Dark Spawn enemies have one Wound. Hunters have three Wounds, with damage affecting their ability to act (see Wounds, page 30).

Locked in Melee

Once two models are in base-to-base contact, they are said to be 'Locked in Melee' until one of them is defeated or disengages. This also applies when an attacking model achieves base-to-base contact with an enemy but lacks sufficient Actions to Attack in the same turn. The following turn, the 'engaged' model must either fight in Melee or attempt to Disengage. The only exception occurs when melee combat models are on either side of an Obstacle, in which case either party may Disengage without suffering a free attack.

Disengaging from Melee

Unless a character has special Skills or equipment, any model attempting to Disengage from a single Melee opponent suffers a Free Attack by the foe, with a -1 to their Dodge Defend roll. A model may not attempt to willfully Disengage from Melee combat with multiple models unless it has special Skills or equipment.

Multiple Opponents in Melee

With the exception of Skills, Traits, or a special Melee weapon, a model can only attack one opponent at a time. Therefore, charging into base-to-base contact with multiple opponents may be possible, but is not advised.

When defending against multiple attackers, a lone model mobbed by enemies suffers a -1 Penalty to their Dodge Defend roll for every attacker after the first; -1 to Dodge Defend roll for two enemies, -2 to Dodge Defend roll for three enemies, etc.

Resolving Mass Melee Mobs

In the event of a real dogfight with multiple combatants, square off Melee fighters into separate one-on-one fights at the beginning of the *next* turn after the initial contact, *before* any further attacks are initiated (this shuffling is free). Should the numbers in a Melee scrum not work out perfectly, square them off as evenly as possible, giving advantage to the Hunters where possible. This makes resolving Melee mobs much easier after the initial shock.

Combat in Low/No Light Conditions

Only Melee combat is permitted in low/no light conditions, unless a Ranged attacker is equipped with a flashlight or a scenario-specific exception (you made up a Darkvision potion for your Case etc.). The bottom line is you can't shoot what you can't see.

Ranged Weapons in Melee

Wielding a Ranged weapon in a Melee situation, either to fire or use as a bludgeon or club, is certainly possible, but is difficult when something is clawing, snarling, or biting at your face. To make a clear distinction between weapon types, there is a -2 penalty to Attack rolls when trying to use a Ranged weapon in Melee combat.

Ranged Combat – The Long Version

Ranged Attacks are resolved following the same basic procedure detailed as Melee Combat, however, the attacker must be equipped with a Ranged Weapon. The attacking model must have sufficient Action Dice in their Action Dice Pool and be able to draw Line of Sight to a target within the weapon's effective range. Weapon ranges are listed with their profile in Section 5 (see pages 46).

Ranged Attack from Elevated Position

In the odd case of an Obstruction between the elevated position and the lower target, the lower Cover/Concealment is reduced by one step as normal, then any remaining Obstructions modify the ranged attack dice roll rather than being removed.

Ranged Attacks from an elevated position reduce the defender's terrain Cover modifier by one step (if applicable). So an Obstruction becomes a clear shot. Concealment becomes an Obstruction, and Cover becomes Concealment.

Direct Versus Indirect Ranged Attacks

Simply put, a direct Ranged Attack is one with a flat, straight trajectory, such as a bullet, a crossbow bolt, a thrown hatchet. An Indirect Ranged Attack is one with an arced trajectory, such as lobbing a Molotov cocktail or Dazzler Contraption.

Technically, the target of an Indirect Ranged Attack does not need to be visible to the attacker, merely within weapon range. This makes the Attack slightly less accurate, incurring a -1 penalty to the Attack roll when the target is visible to the attacker and a -3 when it is not.

Care and Feeding of Grenades

When using any flavor of grenade, designate a target point on the ground or a single enemy model as the intended point of impact, then roll an Action Die of your choice. A result of 4+ is a success (+/- modifiers).

On Target And Drift

If an Attack roll with a grenade is successful, it is considered **On Target**. Center a blast template (size depends on grenade type) over the point of impact. Any model whose base, even in part, falls under the template must make a Dodge Defend roll against damage or the grenade's effects. (a model whose base edge is only *grazed* by the template does not have to make this roll)

If the Attack roll was unsuccessful, the explosive device still went *somewhere*. An unsuccessful grenade toss is considered to have deviated – **Drifted** – off target. To determine the new, adjusted point of impact, roll a single D10. The top face of the die points in the **direction** of the deviation from the original target spot. Next, divide the number shown on that same die face by 2 to get a **distance** in inches.

This direction and distance indicate the degree of **Drift** – the final, unintended point of impact. Center the blast template on this new location and resolve any damage. Remember, a grenade is an equal-opportunity device; a bad throw can injure or kill allies as easily as enemies.

Shadow Rule

A unit is said to be in the '**Shadow**' of a tall Line of Sight-blocking terrain feature if it is within a distance equal to the terrain feature's height. For example, a 3" tall wall has a 3" wide Shadow from its base. This unit **cannot** be targeted by a lobbed grenade from the other side of the terrain item **unless** the Attacking model is also within the same terrain feature's Shadow.

The Shadow Rule reflects the nature of indirect fire and parabolic arcs for abstracted game play. In simple terms, it means a grenade's trajectory can't abruptly drop out of a natural arc.

Also remember that lobbing a grenade at an enemy model or location that is not in the throwing model's Line of Sight incurs a -3 **Penalty** to the roll. Determine any miss using the Drift rules outlined above.

Wounds and The Action Dice Pool

Every successful Hit that was not negated by a successful Dodge Defend roll results in a Wound. While most Dark Spawn adversaries only have one Wound regardless of caste, the Hunters characters can take three Wounds and still function.

However, Wounds have a cumulative effect on the availability of Action Die types and therefore the Hunter's number of available Actions per turn. This means a Hunter's capabilities are increasingly degraded by damage, unless they are healed by a First Aid Kit. Action deterioration due to Wounds is detailed below. Mark wounds on the Hunter's Stat Sheet or with suitably cool tokens near the miniature.

Player Character Injuries and Actions

- No wounds = All die types, Free Move and three Actions
- 1 wound = no D10. May take Free Move and two Actions at D8 and D6.
- 2 wounds = no D10 or D8. May take Free Move and one Action at D6
- 3 wounds = Free Move only.
- 4 wounds = The Hunter is **dead**. Revive them before the end of the engagement or be on the lookout for a new recruit.

Dark Spawn Adversaries Injuries and Actions

As a rule, D6, D8, or D10 caste troops can only take one Wound before they are out of action. In some instances, special abilities or scenario requirements may grant Alpha caste adversaries up to two Wounds. It is recommended players limit two-Wound minions to special occasions or critical narrative junctures.

The final Atrocity enemy is the exception. They have the maximum of three Wounds and degraded performance just like player characters.

Morale Issues – Terror and Dread

Traditional combat between humans is dangerous and stressful. Imagine fighting actual monsters. On occasion, Nightwatch hunters face a particularly horrifying creature and must make a roll to see if the encounter causes them to hesitate – or if it shatters their mind.

Terror rolls are required the first time a Hunter's model comes within 6" and line-of-sight of a Dark Spawn model with the 'Repulsive' Trait. The player must immediately roll their full Action Dice Pool and remove any failed dice (less than 4) from their next activation. The following turn, the revulsion passes and the Action Dice Pool resets to normal.

Again, this Terror roll is required only for the initial encounter and does not need to be repeated for future sightings of that creature or its type and caste during that incident. However, a new Terror roll must be made if another type and caste of Repulsive monster appears.

On the other hand, **Dread** is the deep, soul-shaking anxiety of an existential threat, and it triggers a *Fight, Flight, or Freeze* response. Hunters must make a Dread roll if they suffer a number of Hits equal to or exceeding their Resolve in a single turn (Resolve is equal to half the character's Spirit Primal Attribute). Note that this is Hits, not Wounds, Dread only considers successful Attack rolls, whether the Dodge Defend roll is successful is irrelevant. When that Hit threshold is reached, the Hunter in question must roll a D6 and consult the Dread Table.

Dread Table	
Die Roll	**Result**
1	**They Fight** – The Hunter **immediately** activates and must use all their Action Dice to Attack the nearest Dark Spawn models. This may interrupt the turn sequence. If the character cannot Attack, they must move toward the closest enemy model, regardless of type or caste.
2–4	**They Flee** – The Hunter **immediately** activates and uses all their Action Dice to Move toward the nearest table edge. If their model leaves the game area, they are gone for the remainder of the game. If this occurs during the course of a Case, they are still part of the team but are too traumatized to participate in the next mission.
6	**They Freeze** – Place the Hunter's model prone. The Hunter loses all Action Dice on their next activation and suffers a -2 to all Dodge Defend rolls against Melee attacks while curled up in a fetal position and sobbing uncontrollably. If they are still alive, they will recover the following turn.

Note that some Dark Spawn adversaries have the 'Dreadful' trait, which means their hits count double when calculating the Hits per turn for the purposes of Dread.

Optional Rules: Dark Secret and Odd Touch

In the event that a Hunter falls in battle and dies, the players can simply roll up a new Hunter after the mission and continue investigating the Case. Alternately, the fallen Hunter can be revived after the battle and continue with the Case. However, the trauma will have left them scarred and strangely affected. Hunters revived in this manner are considered to have a Dark Secret and an Odd Touch.

Dark Secret

A grievous, near-fatal wound by a supernatural creature has left the Hunter with a Dark Secret. This is an affliction, addiction, or disorder that influences that Hunter's behavior in both Narrative Scenes and Tactical Engagements, and could have a potentially disastrous effect in the final confrontation with the Atrocity.

Narrative Consequence

Any Hunter harboring a Dark Secret no longer has Favors for the Narrative Scenes in a Case. Their Connection to a specific District remains viable and c an be used, but the buying and spending of Favors is gone. Whether this is the result of a disfiguring injury or emotional and mental distress, they are withdrawn and do not engage with the regular civilian population the way they did previously.

Tactical Consequence

For Tactical Engagements, either select one from the list below or roll a D4 on the table to randomly determine the particular twist to the Hunter's torment and how it affects them on the battlefield.

Dark Secret Table

Die Roll	Dark Secret
1	**Traumatized** – Flashbacks, flinches, and an underlying current of fear runs in the Hunter's mind. Subtract 2 from the character's Resolve and subtract 2 from all Terror rolls.
2	**Bloodthirsty** – Blood for blood, this character is fixated on killing Dark Spawn. Once adversary models are in Line of Sight, the Hunter cannot perform any Action other than to Attack or Move into attacking range when activated, and once they Attack a particular model, they will not stop until it or they are dead.
3	**Cursed** – A werewolf bite, a necrotic wound, or seductive visions, whatever it is, unless the team spends ten Arcana to manufacture a cure, the Hunter risks becoming enthralled to the Atrocity in the final confrontation (simply gather and spend 10 Arcana during Downtime, then declare the antidote administered). If the cure is 'made' before the 6th mission, the Hunter activates as normal. If the cure is not made in time, the Hunter must roll a D6 (free roll) each time they activate during the final mission. On a 4+, they carry on as normal. On a 1–3, they are controlled by the Atrocity that turn and activate as a Dark Spawn with all their Action Dice, weapons, abilities, and Skills. This 'Thrall Roll' is made at the beginning of every turn until either the character or the Atrocity is killed (control can switch back and forth over the course of the game).
4	**Obsessed** – Roll a D6 at the start of every Tactical Encounter. 1–3: The Hunter is consumed with recovering every Clue they can. 4–6: They must gather Arcana. Regardless of their character class or derived abilities, the Hunter may not engage in combat except in self-defense. They will spend all their actions attempting to search Points Of Interest, Portals, or a Nexus.

Odd Touch

The Hunter's brush with death has left them with trauma, yes, but also an Odd Touch; a strange skill or paranormal ability that can be used in the fight against the Dark Spawn. Select one or roll a D4 on the Odd Touch Table.

An Odd Touch is permanent but can be used only once per Tactical Engagement, and its use must be declared at the start of the Hunter's turn. No die roll is necessary. The ability or power is 'activated' simply by the character spending any two of their Action Dice. Their Free Move cannot be used against this cost, but the Hunter may ignore any actions mandated by the Dark Secret one time to use their 'gift' and help their comrades.

Odd Touch Table	
Die Roll	Odd Touch
1	**Whispers in the Blood** – The Hunter's senses extend not merely into occult realms, but the recent past as well. When the Hunter is in base-to-base contact with a Point Of Interest, they may pull one additional Clue from the location using an Interact action, even if it has previously been searched and cleared (consider it missed or overlooked evidence).
2	**Echoes of the Newly Dead** – The character gives voice to the Dark Spawn's recent victims as a profound sense of outrage and loss surges through their being. The Hunter utters a deep groan or wordless shout, and every Dark Spawn model on the board flinches, automatically losing one Action Die from their next activation.
3	**Fiends' Flaws** – In a flash of insight, the Hunter gets a glimpse of their enemy's vulnerabilities and intentions for the next few moments. They call out to their fellows and, for the remainder of that turn, all Hunters receive a +2 bonus to their Attack and Dodge Defend rolls. This is in addition to any other benefits and modifiers.
4	**Step behind the Veil** – The Hunter slips into another dimension for a few brief seconds and may immediately teleport themselves or an ally up to 8" from their current position. Can be used while in Melee and does not incur a Free Attack. However, the destination location (and the friendly model, if used on an ally) must be in Line of Sight to the Hunter.

Rules of Engagement Summary

1. When activated, all Hunters receive a Free Move Action plus an Action Dice Pool of 1D6, 1D8, and 1D10.

2. Dark Spawn Minions use one die type specific to their caste and receive one Free Move plus a number of Actions commensurate with their caste. The final boss, the Atrocity, uses an Action Dice pool similar to a Hunter.

3. Success when attempting an Action is a 4+ (plus or minus modifiers) on an Action Die. Less than a 4 is considered a failure and the Action Die is spent for that turn. Models may continue to activate as long as they have Action Dice left to spend.

4. All Hunters are granted a 'Two Dice Bonus' for specific Actions related to their character class. This means they roll two Action Dice of the same type and can select the better result (also known as 'rolling with advantage').

5. Models may attempt any action so long as they have Action Dice. With the exception of the special Overwatch action, unused Action Dice do not carry over to the next turn. Action Dice Pools are renewed each turn.

6. Hunters can take up to three Wounds, losing their highest Action Die for each successive injury.

7. In general, Dark Spawn minions can only suffer one Wound before being taken out of action.

8. Hunters that are put out of action and not revived before the final turn of a game may either 'retire' that character and create a new Hunter or resurrect them. If they resurrect them, the Hunter loses their Favors (but not their Connections), and rolls a D4 on the D4 Dark Secret and Odd Touch tables.

4 – Dark Spawn

Predatory beasts, insidious demons, ravenous undead, embittered wraiths, and more have terrorized humankind from the dawn of time. Despite the scorn and skepticism of the modern age, your team of misfits is on the front line in a centuries-old war against supernatural threats.

Bear in mind, *Nightmares* is an open-miniature rules set. The following designations are intentionally broad and abstract to suit a wide range of personal preferences and miniature collections. *Your hunt – Your call* is the only hard rule, so you're free to reclassify enemies according to a particular mythos or setting.

Dark Spawn Classification

In *Nightmares*, all adversaries are collectively termed 'Dark Spawn'. There are five classes of otherworldly enemies: the **Restless**, the **Possessed**, the **Cursed**, the **Damned**, and the **Others**. It is recommended players select and collect miniatures around a specific theme as it just looks cooler if the aesthetics are unified.

The **Restless** are undead. Unable or unwilling to depart this mortal plane, they are zombies, ghouls, ghosts, and the like. Depending on your view, vampires can fall in this category as well.

The **Possessed** are afflicted or enthralled mortals, as well as earthly creatures such as bats, wolves, crows, and rats operating under a malign influence.

The **Cursed** are were-creatures, such as werewolves, shapeshifters, and skin-walkers. Dangerous in mortal human form, they are deadly in their transformed state. In addition, any unnatural beasts such as trolls, gargoyles, harpies, or any similar creature removed from its usual time period or habitat fall in this category.

The **Damned** are the creatures of Hell. From imps to hell-hounds to fallen angels, demonic adversaries bear the stench of sulfur and suffering, and a feverish eagerness to inflict the same on humanity.

The **Others** hail from the cold dark void of a dark, chaotic plane of existence. This category encompasses any form of mind-shattering, trans-dimensional, eldritch-type adversary.

> *"And in other news: City Police report there's been another murder on the waterfront, bringing the total to seven in as many weeks. The Mayor's office immediately issued a statement expressing their 'deep concern and tireless determination to apprehend whomever is targeting the most vulnerable members of our proud city.'*
>
> *"Local residents complain the investigation is for show, citing the ongoing lack of police presence and the rising body count. 'It is obvious City Hall doesn't care. If a serial killer had struck at University Square, they'd be dead or in prison by now. If this continues, we're going to take matters into our own hands.'*
>
> *"Police Chief M. Ellis declined to comment further, saying only that 'the department is exerting every effort to hunt down the killer and they take a dim view on vigilantism.'*
>
> *"More as this story develops."*
> *– Channel Seven. Deacon Falls Action News.*

Dark Spawn Castes

Regardless of the classification, the forces of darkness are slavishly hierarchical. Each group is divided into four distinct castes. Each tier is distinguished not so much by appearance as by capability, with higher tier adversaries considerably more experienced and deadly. For example, low-caste Vermin for the forces of the Damned tend to be Imps, while most Hunters consider Zombies to be the Vermin caste when fighting the Restless.

The four castes are **Vermin, Horde, Terror,** and **Atrocity.** The first three are Minion-level enemies. The last one, the Atrocity, is a unique individual similar to a Hunter.

Die Type and Number of Actions

In game terms, each Minion tier is defined by the Die Type they roll when attempting actions and the number of possible actions they can perform. Full details on Actions can be found in Section 3 (page 21).

- **VERMIN** – One Free Move and One Action with a D6
- **HORDE** – One Free Move and Two Actions with a D8
- **TERROR** – One Free Move and Three Actions with a D10
- **ATROCITY** – The final boss. An individual similar to the Hunters with an Action Dice Pool of D6, D8, D10, two Dark Spawn Traits, and one Desecrated Artifact.

Dark Spawn Traits

Even though each caste's abilities are clearly defined, Dark Spawn adversaries can be 'flavored to taste' to suit a specific narrative or range of miniatures. This is done by assigning appropriate Dark Spawn Traits to the models and tweaking their stat lines. There are twelve different Dark Spawn traits that you can mix-and-match to give variety to the things that want to devour your soul or gnaw on your face.

Vermin may select any one trait, Hordes any two, and Terrors any three. The final boss, the Atrocity, can select any two traits, plus one from the exclusive Atrocity list.

> *"I'm telling the truth, swear to God: I saw 'em, just for a second, two men with overcoats and top hats. The old-fashioned kind, like they were in a play or something. But their legs and arms were long and bent all wrong, and they were hunched over, scuttling on all fours, sideways, like crabs."*
> – DFPD Interview. Witness no. 5. 'John S.'

Dark Spawn Trait List

- **Explosive Convulsions** – This Dark Spawn is murderous, even in death; it explodes when killed. Center a small template (3") on the model when it's killed. All models under or touched by it must make an unmodified 4+ Dodge Defend roll or suffer one Wound.
- **Dreadful** – This particular Dark Spawn invokes a deep sense of existential dread, instigating Dread rolls much sooner. Blows from this adversary count double against a Hunter's Resolve.
- **Fast** – Whether it scuttles, slithers, or sprints, it's unnervingly fast. Add 2" to the model's Move Rate.
- **Flight** – As if all those claws and fangs weren't enough, this thing can fly. These enemies can move over terrain items and scenery up to 3" tall. Distance is measured on the ground. The extra inches needed to rise or dive are not counted against their movement rate.
- **Flurry** – Be it volley of spines, blood crystals, or ice shards, whatever it is, whenever this model makes a ranged attack, the target must make two Dodge Defend rolls as though attacked twice.
- **Frenzied** – Whether it's rabid, has an extra set of limbs, or is just unnaturally quick, whenever this model attacks in melee, the target must make two Dodge Defend rolls as though attacked twice.
- **Repulsive** – Hideous, unnerving, and vile, all player character models must make a Terror roll the first time they come within 6" and Line of Sight of this creature.
- **Savage** – The first time in a Tactical Engagement that this Dark Spawn creature moves into melee with a Hunter, it gets a free melee attack roll. This advantage only activates on the initial contact with the Hunter's model and is negated against multiple opponents.
- **Self-Defense** – This creature has a close-range defense mechanism. Melee attackers must always make Dodge Defend roll when they land a successful Hit on this creature, even if the Hit was blocked.
- **Spew** – Scorching fire, acidic slime, revolting ectoplasm, or a cone of soul-sucking dark matter from the void between stars, this model's attacks use the 8.25" Teardrop Spray Template. All models under or touched must make a standard 4+ Dodge Defend roll or suffer one Wound.
- **Swarm** – Applied to a unit with multiple models on a single base, the target of these little buggers' Melee attacks suffers a -1 penalty to their Dodge Defend rolls. This trait is negated if two Hunters are fighting the same swarm unit together.
- **Tenacious** – Usually applied to zombies, but this trait can be given to any particularly stubborn enemy that's hard to kill and just keeps coming. Any Hit except for Aimed Attacks or Natural Crits – Ranged or Melee – simply knocks the model Prone. Prone models suffer a -3 penalty to their Dodge Defend rolls while down. Prone models must expend an Action to get back up on their feet/paws/claws/hooves/tattered spectral robes, and cannot perform any other Action until they do so.

Dark Spawn Move Rate

The default Move Rate for Dark Spawn models is 6". Yes, that's quicker than the most athletic Hunter. Of course, players can adjust adversary speed to suit their tastes, but the higher Move Rate is intentional in order to generate a sense of unnatural danger and tension in a close quarters battle. After all, if monster hunting were easy, then anyone could do it.

Dark Spawn Minion Alphas

When investigating a full Case, the Dark Spawn deployment table calls for an 'Alpha' caste minion at certain intervals. This Alpha is a mini-boss: a special, individual baddie that's more dangerous than the average Dark Spawn, but not an Atrocity-level opponent. Available at every Minion caste, think of it as mid-level management.

Alpha minions are also useful for one-shot games when the story calls for the challenge of a confrontation with an especially dangerous adversary of a particular minion caste. In these cases, make the Alpha model more dangerous by statting it out with two Wounds and assigning it a different trait from its peers, or an additional one if you're feeling confident.

The Atrocity

The Atrocity is the final boss. This is the mastermind behind the terrible crimes the players have been investigating. There is only one Atrocity per Case and they are revealed in the final game of the Case.

The Atrocity is the equivalent of an evil Hunter, having their own Action Dice Pool, any two Dark Spawn Traits, and one signature Atrocity Ability from the list. Note that Atrocities do not receive a Two Dice Bonus for any particular action – they're dangerous enough as is.

Atrocity Ability List

- **Arcane Power** – The Atrocity is an evil spellcaster. Pick two Weaver spells, except for Heal and Revive, and evil-ize them. For example, **Barrier** becomes **Bone Wall** or **Elemental Fury** becomes **Chill Wind from the Grave**. Those spells are added to the Atrocity's arsenal for the game and they may cast them using any Action Die type.

- **Cursed Weapon** – The Atrocity possesses a cane sword forged from volcanic ore, a heavy ring scribed with foul runes, bullets daubed with a heretic's blood, or some other such nefarious weapon. On any Attack Roll that results in a Critical Success that Wounds the target, the weapon inflicts the Burn Condition (the Defender must keep making Dodge Defend rolls at a -2 penalty until they either save or succumb to their injuries). In addition, on any blocked Hit, the Defender must pass a Free roll on their highest die type (4+) or retreat 3" away from Atrocity. (Disengage/Free Hack rule applies).

- **Miasmic Shroud** – A swirling cloak of dark energy, vile fog, or thick smoke, that adds one to all the Atrocity's Dodge Defend rolls against Ranged Attacks and inflicts a -1 penalty to any Melee attacker's rolls.

- **Resurrect Minion** – Good help is hard to find, which is why the Atrocity can bring any of their Dark Spawn minions back to life/un-life. The Atrocity must be within 6" and Line of Sight to the out of action minion model, then roll a success on one Action Die. This ability can be activated as often as the Atrocity needs during their activation and there are out of action minions within range and LOS.

- **Soul Siphon** – Forget winning that 'Boss-of-the-Year' award; this Atrocity can heal themselves by killing a nearby Dark Spawn minion. The model to be sacrificed must be within Line of Sight and 12" of the Atrocity. No dice roll is required; the Atrocity simply 'spends' one of their remaining Action Dice that turn, the minion then dies and the Atrocity's Wound is healed. This can only be done once per turn and cannot be done in lieu of a Free Move.

- **Vampiric Touch** – The Atrocity can heal themselves by wounding a Hunter. The Atrocity must declare their intent *prior* to the Attack Roll. If the Attack is successful and inflicts a Wound on the target, not only is the damage is applied, the Atrocity heals one of their own Wounds. This can only be done once per turn.

Controlling Dark Spawn Models

The biggest challenge in a solo/cooperative game is running the enemy forces. Dice add a randomizing factor, so no action is ever guaranteed to succeed, but the player or players sit in both commanders' chairs with every model and unit visible. You can't surprise yourself here.

In order to side-step the need for flow charts or dice roll tables with dozens of possible 'If-Then' actions and reactions, **Nightmare's** 'Enemy A.I.' focuses on attitude rather than tactics, and establishes four guidelines for Dark Spawn command and control: **Attitude, Target Priority, No Cohesion,** and **Three's Company**.

Attitude Is Everything

Dark Spawn adversaries are malevolent, aggressive, and cunning. They hate you. They want to kill you. They've been hating and killing humans for centuries. They may move on a direct path toward a target, but they're not going to wander blindly into your line of fire or fall for obvious traps. Dark Spawn use cover when possible, they gang up on individuals, and target immediate threats.

Target Priority

Dark Spawn target the most obvious threat. This means they will target the closest visible enemy that they have the clearest Line of Sight to first. If there is only one target, then all creatures in Line of Sight will focus their attention on them. If multiple enemies are present, they will prioritize imminent threats by distance and cover, assigning a minimum of two attackers to each enemy in order of priority.

Target Priority Examples

Three Hunters are investigating a crime scene at Lover's Leap in the State Forest. Four Imps (D6 Vermin) reeking of misery and malice are lurking in the woods, armed with fiery, barbed darts.

Scene 1: Two of the Hunters are in range of the Imps but out of Line of Sight as they are behind an abandoned Ford pickup. The third Hunter was caught in the open in the picnic area. She's in range but hunkered down behind a row of metal garbage cans (in Cover).

When the Imps activate, there's no way they can get a better angle using their Free Move, so despite the Cover modifiers, all four of them hurl flaming darts at her.

Scene 2: Same area, same three Hunters. One Hunter is caught in the open, the second is closer to the fiends but behind some shrubs (Concealment), and the third is farther away, still behind the garbage cans (Cover).

The Imps activate. Two immediately target the Hunter in the open. The next two target the Hunter behind Concealment. The Hunter behind the garbage cans breathes a (shallow) sigh of relief.

Scene 3: One Hunter is hidden behind shrubs (Concealment), while the other two are behind two different types of Cover, garbage cans and a stone firepit. Two Imps will target the Hunter in Concealment, the other two will target the Hunter closest to them in Cover. If both Covered Hunters are equidistant, the Imps will attack the one deemed to be the biggest threat, say the one armed with a Ranged Weapon rather than a Melee one. However, if the Melee Hunter had just killed a fellow Damned or thrown a Pipe Bomb at them, the players/Imps may decide that they are the greater threat at the player's discretion. The Rule of Cool always applies.

No Cohesion

Once adversary models spawn out of a Portal, they're off the leash. Target priority, terrain features, and ease of movement may cause them to move in proximity to one another, but they do not need to stay together and will peel off to attack targets of opportunity.

Three's Company

Whenever possible, Dark Spawn will square off, one on one, until each Hunter has at least one opponent. If there are an odd number of Dark Spawn on the table compared to the number of visible Hunters, then no more than three will gang up on a single target. The rest will move to 'search for' or otherwise gain advantage on the remaining Hunters.

At the end of the day, the game's 'artificial intelligence' will be as smart as the players want it to be. These rules have every confidence that most players will, in fact, respect the guidelines and challenge themselves so that a genuinely hard-fought battle and the coolest possible story unfold on the tabletop.

Multiple Dark Spawn models in close proximity: To streamline play, roll a single die so long as like minion models are bunched together and moving the same direction. Roll and resolve all attack, defense, and separated movement individually.

Sample Dark Spawn Adversaries
Strigoi Adversaries

Sebastian Blōtmonath – Vampire Sire	
Level	**Atrocity:** Free Move plus Action Dice Pool of 1D6, 1D8, 1D10
Move	6"
Armor	4+ on 1D6
Traits	Flight, Tenacious
Signature Ability	Vampiric Touch

Brides	
Level	**Terror:** Free Move plus Action Dice Pool of 1D6, 1D8, 1D10
Move	8" (already adjusted for the Fast trait)
Armor	4+ on 1D10
Traits	Fast, Frenzied, Dreadful

Thralls	
Level	**Horde:** Free Move plus 2D8 Action Dice
Move	8" (already adjusted for the Fast trait)
Armor	4+ on 1D8
Traits	Fast, Savage

Bats	
Level	**Vermin:** Free Move plus 1D6 Action Dice
Move	6"
Armor	4+ on 1D6
Traits	Swarm

Eldritch Adversaries

Da'Gathrx – Baron of the Cold Void between Stars	
Level	**Atrocity:** Move plus 1D6, 1D8, 1D10 Action Dice Pool
Move	6″
Armor	4+ on 1D6
Traits	Dreadful, Repulsive
Signature Ability	Resurrect Minion

Guardians	
Level	**Terror:** Free Move plus 3D10 Action Dice
Move	6″
Armor	4+ on 1D10
Traits	Dreadful, Spew, Tenacious

Spawn	
Level	**Horde:** Free Move plus 2D8 Action Dice
Move	6″
Armor	4+ on 1D8
Traits	Dreadful, Explosive Convulsion

Cultists	
Level	**Vermin:** Free Move plus 1D6 Action Dice
Move	6″
Armor	4+ on 1D6
Traits	Savage

Dark Spawn Summary

1. Enemies are called Dark Spawn.
2. There are five categories of Dark Spawn: the **Restless**, the **Afflicted**, the **Cursed**, the **Damned**, and the **Others**.
3. There are four tiers or castes of adversary: Vermin, Horde, Terror, and Atrocity
4. There are twelve Dark Spawn Traits available to customize adversaries.
5. All adversary models have a Free move plus a certain number of Action Dice available when they activate. Dark Spawn default Move Rate is 6".
6. The three castes of minion enemies (Vermin, Horde, and Terror) each use a particular die type, with higher castes using higher die types. Higher castes also have more chances to act during a turn.
7. All minion caste adversaries have one Wound.
8. Individual Alpha minions may have one more Trait than their caste limit and/or up to two Wounds.
9. Vermin Caste use one D6 and may select one Dark Spawn Trait.
10. Horde Caste use two D8s and select two Dark Spawn Traits.
11. Terror Caste use three D10s and select three Dark Spawn Traits.
12. Atrocity-level adversaries are the final boss. They are an evil character in their own right with a Free Move plus an Action Dice Pool of 1D6, 1D8, and 1D10.
13. Atrocities select any two Dark Spawn Traits plus one from the exclusive Atrocity Attribute list.

5 – The Supply Closet

In any war, you need weapons, armor, equipment, and supplies. This one is no different. The tricky thing about these battles is that you're not fighting people; these are monsters – in every sense of the word. No, they're not poor, misunderstood creatures or some kind of rare, endangered species. They're malevolent, cunning, cruel, and supernatural. Which means you need *more* than guns and body armor.

This chapter details the weapons and equipment required for occult warfare. It's divided into three sections. The first covers **Mundane** items: melee and ranged weapons, protective gear, and a few common but useful articles. The second portion addresses devices of a more **Occult** nature: Contraptions, Concoctions, and Esoterica. The final section covers magical and arcane **Powers**.

Mundane Weapons and Equipment

*Despite wild reports and internet rumors, full-auto firearms are not readily available in the USA. Players are welcome to tweak weapon lists to reflect the laws and norms in their chosen setting.

In *Nightmares*, the Hunters are not considered to be members of some semi-official, covert bureau of paranormal warfare. This means they aren't rolling up to the site of an Incident in an armored personnel carrier, kitted out with full body armor, festooned with silver crucifixes, and toting M4s and holy hand grenades, all while flashing top secret clearance IDs. More likely, they've got a used mini-van, a hiking backpack, and whatever they can hide under their leather jackets. And they've got to talk their way past the police tape.

Listen, the general public gets nervous enough around crazy; they'll panic if they see up-gunned crazy. The last thing a crew of hunters and investigators needs is a SWAT/Armed Response team showing up in the middle of an exorcism.

Out of Sight, Out of Mind is the order of the day. The ideal for any monster hunter team is to be as inconspicuous as possible, so, unless the players decide specifically to be agents in an occult paramilitary division, the weapons, armor, and gear are restricted to those available to civilians*.

Weapon Characteristics

Every weapon is defined by five values:

- **Heft** – Is it Light, Heavy, or Awkward? Can you use it effectively with One-Hand? Does it require Two Hands? Or Two Hands with Effort?
- **Uses Per Turn** – The maximum number of times the weapon can be used during a character's activation.
- **Range** – How far can it go? What is its effective range on the tabletop?
- **Rate Of Fire** – How many times does the target have to make a Dodge Defend roll against each successful Attack? One shot or a flurry of bullets?
- **Damage** – If this hit lands, is it irritating or a world of hurt? Expressed as a negative modifier to target's Dodge Defend roll.

Weapon Heft and Equipment Slots

In *Nightmares*, a weapon's 'Heft' – Light, Heavy, or Awkward – refers not merely to handling, but its weight and encumbrance as well. A Hunter can only carry or hold so many things at one time so, in game terms, this means weapons require a character to use Equipment Slots when bringing them to a Tactical Engagement. Remember that a character's carrying capacity – their Equipment Slots – is linked to their Body Primal Attribute.

- **Light/One-Hand** weapons use one Equipment Slot.
- **Heavy/Two-Hand** weapons use two Equipment Slots.
- **Awkward/ Two-Hand** weapons use three Equipment Slots.
- **Explosive, Smoke, or Gas Grenades** require one Equipment Slot per pair.
- **Molotov Cocktails** take one Equipment Slot each.

Heft applies to each weapon, so a Hunter armed with a chainsaw and a sawed off shotgun needs to use four Equipment Slots to bring them into battle. (3 for the chainsaw, 1 for the sawed off shotgun) This means they need at least a Primal Attribute Body of D8.

Uses Per Turn

This value establishes the maximum number of times a particular weapon can reasonably be wielded or fired during a Hunter's activation with their normal Action Dice Pool. Misses, deflected shots, and blocked swings count toward this ceiling.

However, any additional Action Dice granted by special conditions, such as a spell or elixir, can be used for combat. These special action dice do not carry over to a player's next activation, but they do effectively bypass a weapon's 'uses per turn' restrictions.

Weapon Range

The listed distances are abstracted 'effective ranges' for imaginary conflicts on a 2' x 2' tabletop game area. They are not indicative of actual firearms under ideal conditions, or even certain real world combat situations. The intention behind a short "effective range" value is to mimic the tunnel vision in a tense, frantic, and usually low-light situation.

Except for spray template weapons, ranged attacks may be attempted at up to double the stated range with a -4 penalty to the Attack Roll. This penalty is in addition to any Cover or Obstruction modifiers.

Rate of Fire

How many rounds or hits land on the target? In game terms, this translates into the number of Dodge Defend rolls that target must make against one successful Attack. A cricket bat may bludgeon a zombie, but a chainsaw digs in and starts chewing.

Damage

How much stopping power is behind each round or blow? This is reflected as a negative modifier to the defender's Dodge Defend roll. For example, ghoul shot with a pistol would subtract 1 from their defense roll, however, if they'd been hit with a shotgun at close range, they would subtract 3.

Weapon Categories

There are three categories of weapons: Melee, Ranged, and Thrown. Note that these are intentionally broad; this abstraction is to accommodate a wide variety of implements and firearms in an open-setting, open-miniature tabletop game.

Melee Weapon Table					
Weapon	Heft	Uses/Turn	Range	Rate Of Fire	Damage
One-Hand: Knife, Baton, Machete, Brass Knuckles	Light	3	Melee	1	0
Two-Hand: Bat, Fire Axe, Katana, Sledgehammer	Heavy	3	Melee	1	1
Two-Hand Heavy: Chainsaw, Industrial Wet Saw, other Power Tools	Awkward	2	Melee	2	3

Ranged Weapon Table					
Weapon	Heft	Uses/Turn	Range	Rate Of Fire	Damage
One-Hand: Pistol	Light	3	1"–12"	1	1
One-Hand: Sawn Off Shotgun (break barrel)	Light	2	1"–6"	3 at 1"–3" 2 at 3+"	2 Reload
One-Hand: Uzi, Tech 9, Mac-10	Light	2	1"–12"	2	1 Jam
Two-Hand: Crossbow, Hunting Bow	Heavy	2	1"–12"	1	1 Accurate Reload
Two-Hand: Pump Action Shotgun (Buck-shot shells)	Heavy	2	1"–12"	3 at 1"–3" 2 at 3+"–6" 1 at 6+"	2
Two-Hand: Hunting Rifle (lever action/bolt action)	Heavy	2	1"–24"	1	2
Two-Hand: Flame Thrower/Chem-Sprayer	Awkward	2	Teardrop template	1 Burn	3/all models
Two-Hand: Semi-Auto Carbine, CX4 Storm, Winchester	Awkward	3	1"–24"	1	1

Thrown Weapon Table					
Weapon	Heft	Uses/Turn	Range	Rate Of Fire	Damage
Knives, Hatchet, Shuriken,	Light	Unlimited	1"–6"	1	0
Improvised Explosive, Pipe Bomb	Light (2/slot)	2	1"–12"	1	2/model – SBT
Smoke/Gas	Light (2/slot)	2	1"–12"	1	Varies – LBT
Molotov Cocktails/ Flammable	Heavy (1/slot)	2	1"–12"	1 Burn	3/model –LBT

Note: Mix-n-match menus are the heart of an open miniatures game. Want a spell-slinging Weaver with a sawn-off 12-gauge? Go for it. A bomb-throwing Wright with a katana? Can do.

Yes, certain Skills are confined to specific character classes, Dual Wield, for example. But that's to ensure that Hunters remain distinct and encourage cooperation among team members. The only hard restriction is that Weavers and Wrights cannot use Awkward weapons. Their Relics and Satchels require too much attention and space.

Blast and AOE Weapons
- SBT = Small Blast Template
- LBT = Large Blast Template
- Teardrop = Teardrop, small end at base of firing model

Use the appropriate template to mark the point of impact for blast weapons or the affected area of a spray weapon. All models under or touched by the template must make Dodge Defend rolls. Models whose bases are grazed by the template do not. Thrown indirect AOE blast weapons are subject to the Drift and Shadow rules in Section 3 (see page 30)

Weapon Traits

Accurate

Anyone brave enough to face monsters with a bow and arrow deserves a little something. Hunters with bows or crossbows may add a +1 bonus to a single die when making a Ranged Attack.

Burn

All models under or touched by a Burn weapon template must make a Dodge Defend roll at a -2 penalty and, because of chemicals, acid, or flame, must keep rolling until they either make their Armor save or succumb to their Wounds.

Jam

A rapid-fire, small caliber bullet hose like an Uzi or Mac-10 may look cool, but they're extremely finicky. Any time a natural 1 is rolled during a Ranged Attack, the weapon has jammed. Resolve the Ranged Attack as normal, but two actions must be spent to clear the weapon before it can be fired again, one to clear the jam, the second to reload it. Like 'Reload', the 'Clear' action can be taken in lieu of the player's Free Move. Otherwise, it requires a 4+ Interact Action on any die type.

Reload

Weapons marked with 'Reload' require an Action to, well, reload. This Reload Action can be taken in lieu of the player's Free Move. Otherwise, it requires a 4+ Interact Action on any die type.

Armor or Personal Protective Equipment

Monsters or no, modern hunters and investigators do not wear a helmet, breast plate, and greaves (how medieval). When it comes to personal protection, it's true that some purchase civilian-grade body armor or motocross gear. However, those tend to draw unwanted attention, so most hunters rely on a heavy-duty canvas or a leather jacket to off-set physical damage (black leather trench coats work too).

Not only is work wear much less conspicuous than hockey pads, but its shortcomings can also be offset with small magic amulets or tokens (see Esoterica, page 53).

Base Defense

The base defense for Hunters is a 4+ on a D6. This represents rugged outer wear, boots, and gloves. Any additional, obvious protective gear, such as football pads, body armor, or a surplus riot shield, grants a +1 modifier per item to a player's Dodge Defend roll, but also add cumulative difficulties to Narrative Scenes (see Section 7 for details, page 69).

"This is the third twelve-gauge reloading press I've bought this year. Iron filings, silver shavings, and salt really do a number on the mechanism."
-- Nightwatch Warden, J. Cliche.

Common Equipment

When it comes to fighting monsters, aside from a good weapon and heavy coat, there's a short list of useful everyday items Hunters frequently equip themselves with. The gear below pertains exclusively to Tactical Encounters and can be equipped by any class of Hunter with an open Equipment Slot.

- **Bandages/First Aid Kit** – One-time use. Heals one Wound. Can be applied to self in lieu of a Free Move or to another character with a successful Interact action when in base-to-base contact. Uses one Equipment Slot.

- **Kaiju Energy Drink** – One-time use. Immediately adds 2D6 to the character's Action Dice Pool when imbibed. Extra or unused actions do not carry over to the next activation. Can be consumed in lieu of a Free Move or given to another character with a successful Interact action when in base-to-base contact. Uses one Equipment Slot.
  Side Effect: Crash. The player's entire Action Dice Pool is reduced to D6s for the following activation. The Action Dice Pool resets to normal after Crash.

- **Flashlight/Lantern** – Unlimited uses. If equipped, it automatically grants a +2 to all Search and Extract rolls when interacting with a Point of Interest, Portal, or Nexus. Also allows Ranged attacks with appropriate weapons to a maximum of 12" in Low and No Light conditions. Uses one Equipment Slot.

- **Road Flare/Air Horn** – One-time use. Temporarily distracts opponents. Allows user to Disengage from Melee combat without suffering a Free Attack and Dodge Defend penalty. Disengage by movement of one base width away from enemy model or models. Good for base-to-base contact with up to four enemies. Also, this Disengage benefit applies to any/all allies involved in a melee scrum within 6" of the user. Uses one Equipment Slot.

Occult Items

This portion covers magic artifacts; the specialized items available exclusively to Wrights and Weavers, as well as a short list of common runic tokens collectively known as Esoterica.

- **Wrights** are technicians and chemists who fabricate unusual but useful devices and elixirs to fight supernatural horrors. Termed "Contraptions" and "Concoctions", Wrights carry these items in special bags called Satchels. A Satchel's base carrying capacity is linked to the Wright's Mind Primal Attribute. This can be increased by advances and upgrades over the course of a Case (see Section 8 for details, page 74). A Satchel is considered a 'Light' item and uses one Equipment Slot.

- **Weavers**, on the other hand, are mystics and psychics who channel paranormal energies – what some call spells or divine powers – to combat otherworldly adversaries. Every Weaver carries a personal, sacred item called a "Relic", which acts as a focus and conduit for these primal energies. The base number of spells that can be cast by a Weaver through a Relic is determined by that Weaver's Spirit Primal Attribute. This number can be increased by advances and upgrades over the course of a Case (see Section 8 for details, page 74).

- **Esoterica** are small decorative items marked by magical runes. These can be clay beads, engraved amulets, etched glass, or carved wood, bone, or stone charms. The shape and material are irrelevant, the arcane sigil is what grants a one-time benefit to the wearer. These can be purchased and worn by any character class.

Contraptions

Imagine a paranormal version of a dog whistle, a mousetrap, or mosquito repellant, and you're moving in the right direction. Wrights are support specialists whose inventions can turn what was about to become an evisceration into an exorcism. Only a Wright can handle these items and must roll an Action Die to deploy them. However, they receive their class-related Two Dice Bonus when doing so.

Lure

A package of giblets soaked in God-knows-what. Or a smudge stick made with a child's hair, black widow spider silk, and sage weed. Whatever it is, it draws all Dark Spawn in the mission area toward its location. Lures can be placed with an Interact Action or thrown like a grenade using a Ranged Attack. The attraction effect is powerful but limited to the Dark Spawn phase of the turn in which it is deployed.

Note: When thrown like a grenade, Lures, Snares, Repellant, and Dazzlers are subject to the Indirect Ranged Attack rules in Section 3 (page 28). However, a Wright's Two Bonus Dice applies when handling these devices.

Place a token at the Lure's location. Remove it at the start of the next run. During the next activation, all Dark Spawn models must use their Free Move and all Actions to Move toward the Lure on a direct path (or as close as possible).

Lures will not draw off any Dark Spawn in Melee or within 1" of a Hunter. Any Dark Spawn that comes within 1" of a player character while moving toward a Lure will halt there and end its turn, regardless of any remaining available Actions. Dark Spawn behavior reverts to normal once the lure has been removed.

If multiple Lures are deployed in the same turn, Dark Spawn models will move toward the closest one.

Snare

An area effect device, this item freezes all Dark Spawn models in place during the turn in which it is deployed. A snare can be placed with an Interact Action or thrown like a grenade using a Ranged Attack. Place a token to note the location, then center the 5" Large Blast Template on the marker. All enemy models under or touched by the template cannot move for the remainder of the turn. Mark all affected models with a chit or token. All snared or frozen Dark Spawn Models suffer a -2 penalty to their Dodge Defend rolls, but may perform any other action, such as make a Ranged Attack.

Snare markers are removed at the beginning of the next turn and all area effects end.

Repellant

Garlic, Iron Filings, Monkshood, similar to a snare, this is another Area Effect device. Repellant can be placed with an Interact action or thrown using a Ranged Attack. Place a token at the target location, then center the 5" Large Blast Template on the marker. All Dark Spawn models under or touched by the template must make an about face and Move in a straight line directly away from the center of the blast. Repelled Dark Spawn models must use their Free Move and all available Actions to flee, moving around any large terrain they cannot pass through, stopping only if they come within 1" of a player character model or reach the edge of the game area.

The repelling effect lasts only for the turn in which it is used. Remove the repellant marker at the beginning of the next game turn.

Dazzler

A flashbang for monsters. Dazzlers must be thrown using a Ranged Attack. Place a token at the target location, then center the 3" Small Blast Template on the marker. All Dark Spawn models under or touched by the template must make a Dodge Defend roll at a -4 penalty.

A success allows them to act normally. A failure means they are stunned and lose all their Action Dice for the next activation. Place all stunned enemy models prone to mark their condition. Stunned Dark Spawn suffer a -4 penalty to any subsequent Dodge Defend rolls that turn. Any surviving Dark Spawn models must roll to regain their footing on the next run (4+ on their caste's action die).

Concoctions

Potions, elixirs, doses, nips, whatever you want to call them, they smell foul and taste medieval. Only the good Lord and the Wright know the ingredients – and neither of them want to talk about it. They work though, and that's what matters. Potions can be imbibed by a Hunter in lieu of their Free Move action, or they can be applied or given to another Hunter with a successful Interact action while in base-to-base contact.

Healing

A shot of thick and bitter syrup that heals up to two Wounds and restores all applicable action dice. Alternately, it may be given to an injured party with only one wound, in which case the additional healing power grants the recipient an extra Free Move action that turn, which must be taken immediately if the character has already activated, or during their upcoming activation. This does not carry over to the next turn.

Soothe

Burns all the way down and makes your eyes water. This draught of liquid courage provides a sense of confidence that borders on invulnerability. It immediately removes any and all Terror or Dread effects, as well as granting a +1 bonus to the recipient's Dodge Defend rolls that same turn.

Revive

Everyone who has ever imbibed this potion gags when they recall its taste, but at least they're alive to remember it. This Concoction gets any Out of Action ally back on their feet. However, it only restores them to medium health, leaving them with one Wound (Free Move plus 1D6 and 1D8 Action dice). The character's remaining Wound can be healed, and the lost D10 Action Dice recovered, by using mundane First Aid Kits or a Healing spell or potion.

Speed

A slug of what tastes like lime-flavored battery acid. It leaves the user's hands shaking and nerves jangled. A swig adds a +2 to the user's Move action rolls and adds an additional 2" to their Move Rate during the turn in which it was taken. The effects do not carry over to the next activation.

> *"Father O'Malley caught me filling my canteen with holy water from the font last Sunday. On the spot, I mumbled up a weak story about an ailing grandmother battling cancer, and now he wants to visit her in hospice."*
> *– Nightwatch Weaver, S. Jones.*

Esoterica

Esoterica is the generic term for small amulets, charms, and talismans infused with a sliver of arcane power. Worn on the hunter's person or attached to their clothing, they are typically inscribed with a magic rune or sigil that provides a specific, single-use benefit to the wearer.

There are five types of common esoterica and Hunters may equip up to two on their person. All five kinds are available to any character class (simply mark them on the Hunter's sheet). Esoterica do not use Equipment Slots but they crumble, vanish, or otherwise become inert after use. New pieces can be purchased between missions (see Section 8, page 74).

To 'use' esoterica, the player simply declares their intention at the pertinent moment during play. No Action roll is required. The item's power goes into effect immediately and the token is 'spent' and removed from the Hunter's sheet.

Granite's Fealty

Allows wearer to shrug off an injury caused by a physical blow or projectile. To be used after a failed Dodge Defend roll, the Hunter may ignore one Wound. Does not work against Dark Spawn magical attacks.

Horizon's Calm

A glimpse of immense perspective grants immunity against the effects of Terror or Dread. Used when in-game conditions trigger the need for either, the amulet shatters and the character is considered to have automatically passed the required roll.

Weasel's Twist

A token inscribed with this glyph allows the wearer to slip out of Melee with up to three enemy models without being subject to Free Attacks. This 'Free Disengage' means the Hunter must immediately move half their Move Rate directly away from their Melee opponents. They cannot come into base-to-base contact or move into Melee combat with another enemy model. If such a Move is impossible (the Hunter is cornered against terrain, for example) then they cannot use this item.

Bear's Rage

A momentary surge of animal ferocity, this token infuses a Hunter's next physical attack with additional accuracy and damage. This boost can only be applied to an imminent physical attack (Ranged or Melee) and must be declared prior to the Attack roll. Grants a +2 bonus to the Attack roll as well as a -2 penalty to the target's Dodge Defend roll. The token's power is spent, regardless of the Attack's success.

Moirai's Benison

A complex sigil that appears to change subtly at each glance. This talisman allows the wearer to reroll any single, failed Action Dice roll. The player must abide by the result of the second roll. In the case of a Two Dice Bonus action, both dice may be rerolled.

Magic or Arcane Powers

Be it via incantations, prayers, or psychic powers, drawing on paranormal energy and directing it to a specific effect falls under different names and disciplines. For the sake of brevity, the generic term 'spell' is used here and any debate on their source is better saved for times when something isn't trying to gnaw your face off or claw your heart out of your chest like a cereal box prize.

Only Weavers can channel arcane power in this manner and, even then, it is focused through a physical conduit, a personal item known as a 'Relic'.

Each Weaver's Relic is unique and associated with their particular arcane discipline and worldview.

The item can be something as common as a family Bible, as eclectic as a Haitian voodoo fetish, or a contemporary novelty like a reproduction wand made of holly and a faux phoenix feather (or a hand-copied portion of the Rig-Veda, a gaudy ring that belonged to an older aunt, a statue of an ancient Canaanite fertility goddess, you get the idea). A Relic is considered a 'Light' item and uses one Equipment Slot.

Relic Charges

A Weaver's ability to cast spells is linked to their Spirit Primal Attribute. Once set, this core attribute cannot be changed. However, spellcasting is also defined by their Relic Charge. If the character's Spirit Primal Attribute represents their willpower, character, and innate connection the spiritual dimension, then Relic Charge is like the chambers in a Colt revolver. Over the course of a game, each spell cast is deducted from the Weaver's Relic Charge. Once the Weaver's Relic Charge has been depleted, the Weaver cannot cast any more spells that game. A Weaver's Relic 'recharges' automatically between missions. A Weaver may upgrade their Relic's 'efficiency' to improve its Relic Charge over the course of a Case to increase the number of spells they can cast.

Misfires

Even though Weavers receive the Two Dice Bonus when attempting to cast spells, be aware that failed spellcasting attempts – misfires – still use a Relic's charges, regardless. Occult effort was expended, so a Charge was spent, whether or not the Weaver succeeds (choose your opportunities isely and roll well).

> *"This is the second time this week I've found the lights on in the archive and the door unlocked. It's also come to my attention that not one but two of the Babylonian tablets are missing. They must be returned immediately. If the Directors find out, it'll be all our heads. Not just mine."*
> – *City Museum, Antiquities Department. Internal Memo.*

Casting Spells

There are eight Weaver spells. All spells are available to every Weaver at any point during a Case. However, some spells are Weighted, meaning additional Charges can be spent to boost or improve that their effects. All spells have a minimum Charge cost of one.

Even though only one roll of the player's Action Dice is needed to cast a particular spell, the Weaver must declare the spell's Weight (the number of Charges they are expending to empower it) before they make their roll.

Note that the spells listed below have generic names. Players can, of course, flavor the terminology according to their particular setting; the emphasis here is on the effect rather than specific jargon.

Example: Sister Margaret with her D10 Spirit can cast five spells during a game. Early in a Tactical Engagement, an enraged phantom comes howling toward her and she picks up her D8 Action Die to utter an imprecatory orison. She decides to cast 'Arcane Bolt' and declares its Weight to be two Charges. Her Relic now has three Charges' remaining for the rest of this encounter.

A Weaver, she gets her Two Dice Bonus and rolls two D8s, taking the better result. She gets a 3 and a 7, giving her a success. The angry phantom must now make a single Dodge Defend roll with a -2 penalty. If Sister Margaret had rolled less than 4 on both dice, she would have failed the casting roll. Regardless of the result, the two Charges would still be spent from her Relic Capacity for the Incident.

Spell List

With the exception of Shockwave and Elemental Fury, all spells have a 12" range. However, spellcasting is not considered a traditional Ranged Attack, so terrain penalties do not apply. However, the Weaver must have Line of Sight to their target.

Heal

Weight 1–3. Knits bones, staunches bleeding, and closes lacerations. A Heal spell can remove up to three Wounds on a Hunter, including the caster, depending on the number of Charges spent in the casting (one Wound per Charge). **Cannot** revive an out of action ally.

Revive

Weight 2. This spell brings an out of action ally back from death's door. The revived character is restored to low health with two Wounds (allowing a Free Move plus 1D6 Action dice). The injured character's remaining Wounds can be healed, and the lost D8 and D10 Action Dice recovered, by using mundane First Aid Kits, the Heal spell, or a healing concoction.

Empower Ally

Weight 1–3. The Weaver imbues an ally and their weapon with supernatural power for a single attack, either Melee or Ranged. The spell grants a bonus to the ally's next attack roll equal to the Weight of the spell and penalizes the target's Dodge Defend roll by the same value. This boost applies to physical attacks only and a Weaver may not cast this spell on themselves.

Barrier

Weight 1. This places a temporary magic wall 4" wide, 4" tall, and 0.5" thick anywhere in range, orientated as the caster desires. This barrier blocks all movement – ground based or flight – plus all Ranged Attacks through the affected area until the start of the following turn.

Arcane Bolt

Weight 1–3. The Weaver sends a bolt of arcane power at a single target. The target's Dodge Defend suffers a penalty equal to the Weight of the spell.

Shockwave

Weight 2. Center the 5" Large Blast Template on the Weaver. All models, both allies and enemies, on the ground or in flight in the area of effect immediately fall to the ground. Prone models suffer a -4 penalty to their Dodge Defend rolls while down. Prone models must expend an Action to get back up on their feet/paws/claws/hooves/tattered spectral robes, and cannot perform any other Action until they do so.

Elemental Fury

Weight 1–3. The Weaver releases a surge of raw, primal energy from their hands. Place the narrow point of the 8.25" teardrop template at the base of the caster. All models under or touched by the template (not grazed) must make a Dodge Defend roll with a penalty equal to the Weight of the spell.

Déjà Vu

Weight 1–3. Cast only on an ally, the recipient may activate a second time that turn. With a Weight of 1, it restores the Hunter's Free Move plus their D6 Action Die. With a Weight of 2, it restores their Free Move, plus their D6 and D8 Actions Dice. With a Weight of 3, it restores their Free Move and all their Action Dice. Déjà Vu can only be cast on an ally that has already activated that turn – the Hunter activates a second time but never back-to-back.

Supply Closet Summary

1. The Hunters are civilian vigilantes and unofficial monster hunters. As such, they make an effort to be inconspicuous. Weapons are restricted to civilian small arms. Armor is usually rugged workwear bolstered by small occult tokens or runes.

2. Weapons are defined by five factors: Heft, Uses Per Turn, Effective Range, Rate Of Fire, and Damage

3. Equipped weapons use a character's Equipment Slots. Light = One, Heavy = Two, Awkward = Three.

4. Mundane Supplies are available to any character class and take one Equipment Slot per item.

5. Occult items are largely confined to the Wright's Contraptions and Concoctions, and the Weaver's Relic. Initially, a Wright's Satchel Capacity and a Weaver's Relic Charge are determined by their Primal Attribute stats. However, the 'efficiency' of those special devices can be increased over the course of a Case.

6. Common occult items available to all character classes are known as Esoterica. These are small rune-etched tokens, charms, or badges that grant one-time benefits to the wearer. Up to two Esoterica can be worn at one time. They do not take Equipment slots. They are destroyed or otherwise rendered inert when used.

Note that a Weaver's powers are formidable but finite, especially in the early stages of a Case. They require fair amount of finesse to run, plus a good share of luck. It's a good idea to have a Warden nearby to act as a bodyguard to keep them from getting swarmed by monsters.

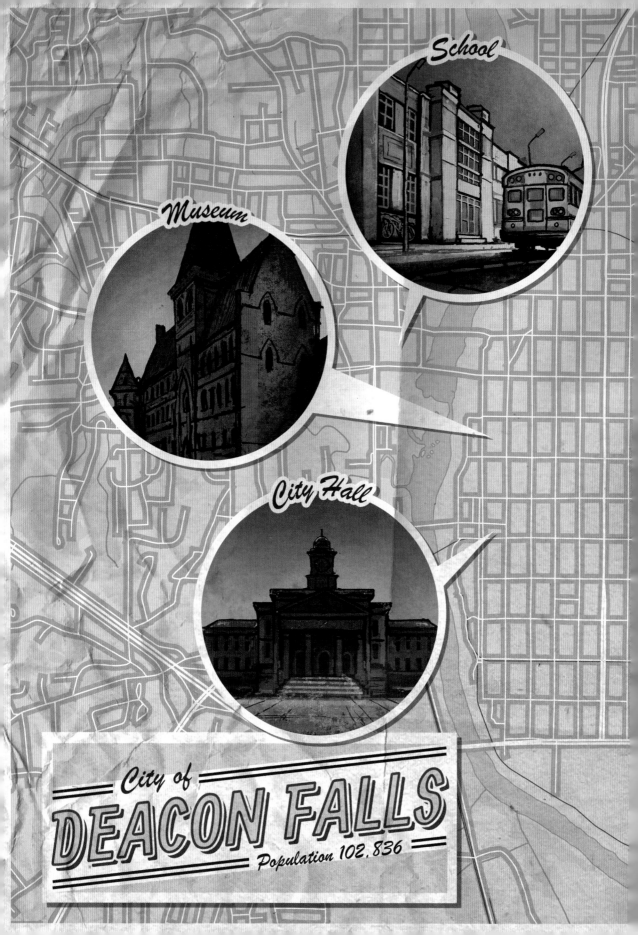

6 – Narrative Scenes

Cue The Scary Music

A key part of *Nightmares* is atmosphere; we're talking *occult* investigation and *supernatural* warfare, after all. It's reasonable that your team of monster hunters will end up in some pretty creepy places, such as at the docks after midnight in a thick fog; in the hospital morgue fending off the antiseptic chill and eerie stillness; creeping among the tall stacks and hard shadows of the city library after-hours; or perhaps following strange tracks in the deep woods of the state park. And of course, there's always graveyards...

One Mission, Two Parts

Each game of *Nightmares* has two components – a Narrative Scene to set the stage and a Tactical Engagement to resolve the action. As a tabletop wargame, the emphasis is on the second portion, but whether you're playing a single, pick-up mission, or running a full Case, Narrative Scenes are part and parcel of *Nightmares*. In a one-shot, they give context to the combat. In a full Case, they generate a storyline and create plot points for the campaign.

Narrative Scenes are the segue to the imminent battle, the 'cut-scene' that adds a sense of immersion for your game group. In practical terms, the outcome of Narrative Scene determines the quantity of evidence, the quality of enemies, and any advantages or disadvantages for character deployment. The story portion shapes the monster hunters' encounter on the battlefield.

Narrative Scenes Use Primal Attributes

Before going further, it's important to note that, during Narrative Scenes, players reference their character's Primal Attributes to resolve any social, intellectual, and non-combat, physical challenges. The specifics are below but, for now, know that if a player wants to perform a feat of strength or agility, they refer to their **Body** stat and die type. If there is reasoning or investigation required, then they use their **Mind** stat and die type. Want to bluff, intimidate, or flirt? Then check the character's **Spirit**. Success at a given task requires a roll of 4+ on the relevant die type. Less than 4 is a failure.

Four Questions

To generate a Narrative Scene, four questions need to be answered: **What? Where? Who?** and **When?** Details are below and the tables in Section 6 (see page 62) can be used to help you find the answers.

The What – An Inciting Incident

Vigilante monster hunters and self-taught paranormal investigators don't respond to every vicious crime; that's what the police are for. Something about a particular event has to strike them as being on the *unnatural* side of wrong. Strange voices, bestial sounds, an unusual mark or wound, details in the reports that defy logic, these are the sort of hints that suggest that something's *different* about a particular event. Fabricate your own terrifying event or look at Table A for suggestions.

Admittedly, many of these incidents are false alarms. For example, it could be that an eyewitness was drunk, high, or exaggerating; it was the work of an unusually brutal, disturbed criminal, or the mundane felon was trying to be clever or misleading. It's when the report wasn't hyperbole or an over-active imagination that the situation gets interesting*.

Read: "Oh god, oh god, we're all going to die."

The Where and The Who – Deacon Falls

All of us know you can have a nightmare anywhere. In an open-world, open-miniature ruleset like this, players can set their games wherever and whenever they want. The fictional city of Deacon Falls referenced in this section offers an example of an investigation setting. That's all. A generic locale, Deacon Falls has six districts, each with a distinct backdrop and demographic. This Anycity, Anywhere is also populated by eight major NPC (non-player character) organizations. These are all outlined in broad strokes to accommodate player imagination and a wide variety of miniature options.

The names in your game scenarios may be different, but in meta-terms, Districts and NPC Organizations are critical factors in determining Narrative Scene challenges and consequences. See below and reference Tables B and C.

Deacon Falls Districts

- **Downtown** - City Hall, Hospital/Morgue, Police and Fire Stations, News Media Outlets, City Park.
- **University Square** – Universities, Museums, Library, Dormitories, Fraternity/Sorority Houses
- **Suburbs** - Neighborhoods, Schools, Malls
- **Estates** – Gated Communities, Mansions, Parks, Golf Courses, Country Clubs, Yacht Clubs
- **Waterfront** - Docks, Warehouses, Dive Bars, Brothels, Cheap Motels, Pawn Shops
- **Outskirts** – State Park, Summer Camp, Lake Resort, Observatory, Cemetery

Deacon Falls NPC Organizations

- **City Officials** – Mayor, Councilors, Committee and Department Heads, Business and Financial Leaders
- **Academia** – Professors, Teachers, Academic Staff, Students, Librarians, Museum Curators
- **Suburbanites** – Families, Shop Owners, Retail Workers, Blue-collar Tradespeople
- **Affluent** – Corporate, Financial, and Tech/Industrial Business Owners, CEOs, Trophy Spouses
- **Criminal Element** – Dealers, Pimps, Prostitutes, Pickpockets, Gangers, Con-Artists
- **City Workers** – Department of Public Works Staff, Sanitation and Maintenance Crews, Fish & Game and Park Service Personnel
- **First Responders**: Police, Firefighters, Paramedics (not associated with any single district)
- **News Media**: Reporters and Journalists for Television, Internet, or Print News Media, (not associated with any single district)

The When – Time on the Scene

As in *'How soon after the mysterious incident or horrible crime does the team arrive on site'*? Are you the first ones there, dealing with shocked witnesses and baffled bystanders? Is the area already cordoned off with Police Tape and flashing lights? Or did you and your fellow Hunters pull up just as the last ambulance pulled away and forensics is done dusting for prints and tracking dirt all over the scene?

Is the Incident site **Fresh**? **In Progress**? Or growing **Cold**? When you arrive determines who you encounter on your way in, and the quality and quantity of the things you find. Check Table D for details.

The How – Narrative Scene Specifics

To answer the four 'W' questions, (What, Where, Who, and When) players should look over the four tables below and either pick one from each that fits their storyline, and terrain, and miniature collection. Or players can roll the appropriate die type to generate a (seemingly) random string of events. For one-shots, roll on all four tables. For a full, six Incident Case, it's only necessary to roll on Table A at the beginning, then tables B, C, and D in-between games.

Narrative Scene Tables
Table A: What?

To kick off your nightmare with its own special cascade of horror and supernatural warfare, one player should roll a D4 and check the table below.

Table A: What?	
D4 Roll	**What in God's Name is Going on Here?**
1	Unnatural Phenomena – An eerie presence, sightings of strange creatures or shadowy figures, the appearance of mysterious symbols – a series of unsettling incidents and unease is growing by the day. The police have no solid leads, but you feel something stirring in the dark; a malevolence working toward some horrid end or waiting for the opportune moment to strike.
2	Serial Killings – A string of gruesome murders. Each crime scene is a horrifying and savage mess. Ruthless, sadistic, ritualized, there are traces of dark arcana but no tangible evidence. The only certainty is that someone died a very nasty death. The police won't admit it, but even they sense something unnatural is going on. Whoever or whatever it is will strike again unless you stop them.
3	Thefts – Things are going missing; artifacts from the museum's antiquities section, rare manuscripts from the library's secure archives, a family heirloom from the old country, and that odd souvenir Grandpa brought back from the war. Whatever they are, they're disappearing one after the other and you have a nagging sense something very bad will happen if you don't get them back.
4	A Series of Disappearances – Celebrities, old-money scions, college students, the homeless, hikers; someone or something is targeting certain types of people. There's no blood, no bodies, no witnesses – they seemed to have vanished into thin air. The investigating detectives have no leads but you recognize the work of Dark Spawn when you see it. Who or what is taking these people? Why? That's what you intend to find out.

TABLE B: WHERE?

From stately mansions to crumbling tenements, from dive bars to board rooms, evil lurks in darkness and there are shadows everywhere. Where did this particular Incident take place?

Table B: Where?	
D6 Roll	**Where Are You?**
1	Downtown – City Hall, Hospital/Morgue, Police and Fire Stations, News Media Outlets, City Park.
2	University Square – Universities, Museums, Library, Dormitories, Fraternity/Sorority Houses.
3	Suburbs – Neighborhoods, Schools, Malls.
4	Estates – Gated Communities, Mansions, Parks, Golf Courses, Country Clubs, Yacht Clubs.
5	Waterfront - Docks, Warehouses, Dive Bars, Brothels, Cheap Motels, Pawn Shops.
6	Outskirts – State Park, Summer Camp, Lake Resort, Observatory, Cemetery.

TABLE C: WHO?

It's a big town filled with all kinds of people who travel wherever they need for business or pleasure. Who are the bystanders crowding the scene?

Table C: Who?	
D6 Roll	**Who's There? Bystanders and Witnesses**
1	City Officials – Mayor, Councilors, Committee and Department Heads, Business and Financial Leaders.
2	Academia – Professors, Teachers, Academic Staff, Students, Librarians, Museum Curators.
3	Suburbanites – Families, Shop Owners, Retail Workers, Blue-collar Tradespeople.
4	Affluent – Corporate, Financial, and Tech/Industrial Business Owners, CEOs, Trophy Spouses.
5	Criminal Element – Dealers, Pimps, Prostitutes, Pickpockets, Gangers, Con-artists.
6	City Workers – Department of Public Works Staff, Sanitation and Maintenance Crews, Fish & Game and Park Service Personnel.

Don't worry if Where and Who don't correlate in typical or expected ways; districts and demographics don't match all the time. Rich kids from the Estates could be having a wild night on the Waterfront. So could City Officials. A garbage truck could be emptying dumpsters at University Square, or a gaggle of professors could be on a nature hike in the State Forest. The narrative possibilities are endless.

TABLE D: WHEN?

Whether it's a tip from a friendly reporter or an intercept on the police scanner, how quickly did the team grab their gear and roll?

Table D: When?	
D6 Roll	**Disposition On Arrival**
1	**Cold** Bystanders and First Responders are present on site. 2 Challenges. 3 Points Of Interest. NPC vigilance is Reduced: Negate any 1 failed Primal Attribute roll.
2	**In Progress** (Critical) Bystanders, First Responders, and News Media are present on site. 3 Challenges. 4 Points Of Interest. NPC vigilance is Heightened: Negate 1 successful Primal Attribute roll during the first Challenge.
3	**In Progress** (Sensational) Bystanders and News Media are present on site. 2 Challenges. 4 Points Of Interest NPC vigilance is Standard: Roll Challenges as normal.
4–5	**In Progress** (Secured) Bystanders and First Responders are present on site. 2 Challenges. 4 Points Of Interest. NPC vigilance is Standard: Roll Challenges as normal.
6	**Fresh** The blood is still warm and sticky. Traumatized Bystanders are present on site. 1 Challenge. 4 Points Of Interest, each with 2 Clues. NPC vigilance is Reduced: Negate any 1 failed Primal Attribute roll. Increased Dark Spawn activity: 1 Alpha Dark Spawn added to each wave on Turn 1 and Turn 2.

Using The Narrative Scene Tables

- Roll 1D4 on Table A to see **What** happened.
- Roll 1D6 on Table B to determine **Where** it happened.
- Roll 1D6 on Table C to see **Who** is at the Scene (bear in mind, the number of NPC organizations on site equals the number of Challenges the team must deal with before they gain access).
- Roll 1D6 on Table D to see **When** you arrive.

Example A

A roll of 3 on Table A and 4 on Table B yields 'A Theft in the Estates'. Next, a 1 on Table C and a 5 on Table D mean a City Official has been robbed (let's say it was the Mayor). The situation is In Progress. Bystanders are family and/or friends who are currently with the police. No one was hurt or killed, so the situation is tense but routine. The crew arrives and parks one street away to avoid being spotted.

Example B

A roll of 4 and 5 on Tables A and B mean there have been 'A Series of Disappearances on the Waterfront'. Next, rolls of 5 on Table C and 6 on Table D means the only people present are local street species. They are shocked and terrified however, because who or whatever did it, is still around. The scene is Fresh.

Challenges, Solutions, and Group Rolls

Details from Tables B, C, and D are here to provide flavor for your Case's storyline, but a Narrative Scenes' function is to establish the Hunters' access and disposition in the upcoming tabletop battle.

Challenge = Obstacle

Depending on the results of the **Who, Where,** and **When** rolls, Narrative Scenes will contain between one to three Challenges. Even though they're equated with the number of NPC Organizations on site, think of Challenges more as puzzles or predicaments that need to be addressed, not simply people you need to shove, swindle, or seduce. These are scene-related problems and obstacles that your crew must navigate.

Depending on the circumstances, the Hunters may be trying to talk their way past the police tape, hacking an electronic lock on the gate to a country club, or fooling the museum janitor into surrendering the key to the service elevator. Locations and bystanders are there to spark players' imagination, the specifics are left to the players. Whatever you come up with, what's important is that each NPC group on site generates one narrative Challenge.

Solutions – Three Methods

Because Challenges are non-combat problems that are resolved using the characters' Narrative Mode Primal Attribute stats, they can be addressed one of three ways:

- **Physical** – Force or sneak your way in. These kinds of actions use the **Body** stat and die type.
- **Reason** – Investigate or argue your way on site. This relates to the **Mind** stat and die type.
- **Charm** – Cajole, Flirt, or Bluff your way past the problem. Use the Hunter's **Spirit** stat and die type.

All Together Now – Group Rolls

To address a Narrative Scene Challenge, players discuss and decide on a single course of action to solve each one. This solution must use one of the three methods: physical, intellectual, or moral/temperament.

Funny or serious, logical or absurd, cool or idiotic, it's up to the players to assess the Narrative Scene's details and come up with a plan in an open, round table discussion; for example, "We're going to jimmy the back window open and climb in quietly"; "We're going to lie to the doorman and say we're insurance adjusters sent to assess the damage"; or "We're going to convince the biker gang it's better if we check out the camp site first."

Once the solution has been decided and paired with a challenge, then every character contributes one die of the relevant Primal Attributes – the type associated with that course of action – and the players make a single Group Roll. For example, four Hunters trying to force the back door means a Body die from each player. The same four reminding the rookie patrolman how they tipped him off to a serial mugger a week prior would mean four Mind dice. Every 4+ is a success and each result less than 4 is a failure.

Tally the results of each Group Roll. More successes than fails means the Group Roll is a **Win**. An equal number of successes to fails is a **Draw**. More fails than successes is a **Loss**. This procedure must be done for each Challenge in the Narrative Scene, and each method – Physical, Reason, Charm – can only be used once; if you're facing three Challenges, you can't Charm your way past all three problems or groups.

Players do not have to attempt all methods or try them in any order – obviously, the team wants to optimize their best die types when confronting Narrative Challenges – but once a method has been decided, the team must abide by the results of the Group Roll.

Tally All Results

Once all required Group Rolls have been made and the results tallied, calculate the final result. Each Win counts as +1, Draws count as 0 and every Loss counts as a -1. The final value of the sum of the Group Rolls determines how and where the Hunters deploy at the start of the upcoming Tactical Engagement. A net positive total yields an advantage, a total of 0 means standard deployment, and a net negative causes disadvantages.

Example: A party is at University Square with Academics, Police, and Media on site, meaning they must undertake three Narrative Challenges. They try to sneak their way (Body) around the cordoned crime scene, then bluff past the crowd (Charm) onto the campus quad, and, lastly, convince someone (Mind) to let them go to the third floor where the weird 'accident' occurred. The Group Rolls yield a Win at sneaking (+1) and a Draw on the bluff, (0) but they fumble their arguments and get a Loss. (-1)

Their final total is 0 (+1 + 0 + -1), which means they will start the upcoming battle in a standard deployment disposition. With a net positive result, the crew would go in with an advantage. With a net negative, they'd be facing monsters at a detriment.

Connections and Favors

Before we explain exactly what a Narrative Win, Draw, or Loss means for your vigilante monster hunters, we need to look at the Hunters' **Connections** and **Favors**, as selected during Character creation. You don't have many but, used correctly, they can mean the difference between victory and defeat.

A Hunter's **Connection** is their association with one particular **District**. It may be their home turf, old stomping grounds, or work territory. Whatever the reason, this person has intimate knowledge of its people, streets, shops, and alleys, and so has an advantage whenever they're in that area. A Connection is never exhausted but may be used only once per player per Narrative Scene.

A **Favor** is a debt or obligation owed to a Hunter by a member of one of the NPC **Organizations**. Someone owes them money, their spouses are best friends, they helped them out professionally. For whatever reason, this person is obliged to assist the Hunter one time per Favor. This means Favors are 'spent' when used in a Narrative Scene.

What are they good for?

A character's Connection and Favors can be used in a Narrative Scene Group Roll to convert any one failed die roll into a success. The player has remembered a back way in, reminded someone of an outstanding debt, or otherwise used some kind of leverage or insider knowledge to turn the situation their way. Such considerations can only be 'called in' when an Incident takes place in an applicable District or if the relevant Organization is present on site.

Connections and Favors can be spent after a Narrative Scene Group Roll, and players may spend as many as they want and have on any given Group roll. However, Connections can only be used once per Narrative Scene per player, and Favors are spent and lost when used.

A Connection, although limited to a single area, is never lost or permanently spent, so as long as the Hunter is alive it can be used. On the other hand, Favors are single-use items. They can be replenished and 'bought' using Clues recovered from Point of Interest locations. Every Clue can purchase one Favor. Players must designate which NPC faction they have purchased a Favor with and make a note on their character sheet.

Win = Advantage, Draw = Standard, Loss = Complications

Win

Simply put, if the final result of all Narrative Scene Group Rolls is a net positive value, then the Hunters surmounted the Narrative Scene obstacles deftly and enter the battle at an advantage. The team may assess the layout and character models may deploy from any side of the mission area they desire, up to one Move Action in from the chosen edge. Essentially, they get a Free Move Action head start.

Draw

If the final result of the Group Rolls is a net value of 0, then the Hunters had a hitch or two during the Narrative Scene. Nothing serious but not smooth either. The team of Hunters deploys onto the battlefield per the standard deployment rules – half the team (rounded up) starts in the middle of a randomly determined edge, as determined by a D4 roll (see Section 7, page 71, for details). The other half of the crew starts on the opposite side.

Loss

If the final result of all the Group Rolls is a negative value, then things went poorly. All team members made it to the Incident site, but they arrived scattered, tense, and otherwise confused. Deploy one Hunter from each edge of the game area, in the middle of the edge (12" from the corners on a 2' x 2' game area). If you have more than five Hunters, double up once every side has a model. Also, the characters do not receive a Free Move on the first game turn, and can only use their Action Dice Pool during their first activation.

Too Fussy? Bin it

Don't like the Narrative Scene portion? Think it's too much work or too complicated just to determine deployment? Or that it makes the tabletop wargame part more dangerous? Immersion and tension are sort of the point but, by all means, ignore this section if what you really want is to get minis on the table and start killing things. Simply follow the standard rules in Section 7, page 69, to set up your battlefield.

Narrative Scene Summary

1. Narrative Scenes add flavor and set the stage for imminent combat.
2. Narrative Scenes are defined by four questions: What? Where? Who? When? Roll on Tables A, B, C, and D for specifics.
3. The number of Challenges in a Narrative Scene is equal to the number of NPC Organizations. Challenges are non-combat obstacles the Hunters must address to gain access to the Incident site.
4. Narrative Scene Challenges refer to the Hunters' Primal Attributes and are resolved by rolling the appropriate die type.
5. Narrative Scene Challenges are solved by one of three methods: Physical, Reason, Charm.
6. Players discuss and select whichever method they want when facing a Challenge, but each method can only be used once per Narrative Scene.
7. The details of a Narrative Scene's Challenges are made up by the players and are decided collectively, using Group Rolls of appropriate die type.
8. Connections and Favors can be used once per Narrative Scene to turn the results of any one failed die roll into a success. Connections are never spent. Favors are single-use but can be purchased with Clues.

9. The net value of all Narrative Scene Group Rolls determines the team's deployment in the next battle – positive gives them an advantage, zero means standard deployment, and a negative value leaves them scattered and off-balance.

7 – Tactical Engagements

Research, collect, and catalogue all the occult data and monstrous specimens you want; at some point you've got to fight. That's why the Nightwatch exists. So, whether you're battling monsters in a graveyard, a car park, a creepy mansion, or a bookstore, this section covers the battlefield.

Four Elements

Confrontations in *Nightmares* take place on a 2' x 2' board, known as the mission area. Each mission area is defined by four elements: **Terrain**, **Point of Interest Locations**, **Portals**, and a **Nexus**.

Terrain

In an open-world, open-miniature wargame, your setting and terrain will vary according to your collection and storyline. Obstructions and Cover are important, so it's recommended that players set up at least two scenery items per square foot and add small, appropriate scatter as desired. Too much clutter will slow the game down but lots of open space with clear lanes of fire and movement make for a very fast and bloody encounter, so a medium density mix of large and small items is best.

Point Of Interest Locations

Each Incident site has four Points of Interest (POI), one per square foot. Each POI contains at least one Clue regarding the nature of the crime and identity of the perpetrators, but POI must be Searched to recover the evidence via an Interact Action.

Ideally, POI are associated with small terrain items, such as a locker, a vehicle, a casualty marker, a piece of furniture. If scatter pieces aren't available, use a token or glass stone. Use whatever works best for your table, so long as each location is clearly marked and identifiable. POI should be spaced evenly throughout the game area and at least 8" from any table edge.

Portals

Portals are how and where Dark Spawn adversaries enter the board. Portals are set at each corner of the mission area and should be marked and numbered one through four. Over the course of the game, enemy models will arrive in waves each turn, their entry points randomly determined by two D4 rolls. Portals are also a limited source of Arcana, a potent, otherworldly substance used to upgrade weapons and equipment.

Nexus

Whether you imagine a rift in the veil between dimensions, a node of mystic power, or a strange artifact that acts as a magnet for unnatural creatures, a Nexus is a concentration of arcane energy that's fueling the occult disturbances in the immediate area. Ideally, the Nexus is also associated with a specific item of scenery – something cool and appropriate – but a clearly identifiable marker or token works just as well. Whichever you choose, the Nexus is elusive and doesn't materialize on the battlefield until the player characters gather the proof of Dark Spawn activity. When visible, a Nexus contains an additional Clue and is a potentially unlimited source of Arcana.

Game Turns

Nightmares uses the 'IGO-UGO' turn sequence – one side moves **all** their models and resolves **all** their actions before the opponent acts. Models can be activated in any order, but each model must complete its activation before another can go.

A single game turn is divided into two phases: the **Nightwatch Phase** (the Hunters) and the **Dark Spawn Phase** (the supernatural adversaries). Both phases constitute one full game turn and after both sides have activated all available miniatures, the turn ends and a new one begins.

Monster Hunters First

Nightwatch characters always activate first at the start of a Tactical Engagement. Turns and activations continue back and forth in that order until the Hunters achieve their objectives, retreat off the board, or the turn limit is reached. Once activated, a model must finish all its Actions before another can go.

Six Turn Limit

As mentioned previously, the Hunters are generally running cross-grain to much of modern society. As such, they need to move quickly on the battlefield, so a single Tactical Engagement on a 2' x 2' area is limited to six turns. Nightwatch Hunters need to stay focused in order to recover Clues, gather Arcana, and eliminate monsters.

Victory Objectives

Killing monsters is the job but, in the bigger picture of exterminating supernatural threats, Nightwatch needs to accomplish two goals each mission: first, search the area's POI to obtain a minimum of **Two Clues** and continue the investigation. Second, to locate and shut down the site's **Nexus**. To claim victory, the Hunters must achieve both before the six-turn limit is reached. The Dark Spawn only have to prevent this.

- **Clues** are recovered from Points of Interest. Although game conditions and special Skills may let players find more evidence, in general, each POI yields one Clue.
  Clues can be recovered by any Hunter in base-to-base contact with a POI with a successful Interact (Search) Action on any Action Die. Once cleared of its Clue, a POI becomes part of the landscape. If special conditions or Skills allow for additional Clues may be found, they must be recovered by separate Interact Actions – one Clue per Action.
- An Incident's **Nexus** is its occult energy source. This 'power core' remains invisible until 3 out of 4 of the site's POI have been searched and at least one Clue has been recovered from each (3 POI, not just any 3 Clues). Once those conditions have been met, the Nexus 'appears'.
  To determine where it materializes, number each square foot of the game area and roll a D4. Note the result and place the Nexus scenic or token in a clear area in the center – or as close as possible to it – of the corresponding quadrant.

Deployment

All Hunter models enter the battlefield at the start of the mission from middle point along the edge of the game area. Depending on the Narrative Scene results and the size of the team, this may be from one, two, or even all four sides. If multiple Hunters deploy on the same edge, pack them in as close as possible.

Dark Spawn models enter the game area each turn from two of the four corners, at the Portals. At the start of each turn's Dark Spawn Phase, roll two D4 to determine the entry points and place the appropriate quantity and type of enemy models at those locations. Once they are all in position, they may activate that same turn. This spawning is done at the start of each adversary phase before any current enemy models activate.

The quality of the Dark Spawn enemies depends two factors: the game turn, and how far along the Nightwatch team is in the investigation – i.e. the mission's position on the Case Timeline (see the Dark Spawn Deployment Table and Section 8, page 71, for details).

For one-shot games, select a position on the Case Timeline and use the corresponding quality of enemies.

Dark Spawn Deployment Table		
Game Turn	Dark Spawn Adversaries	Minis per turn
1	2 random corners/1 per portal	2
2	2 random corners/1 per portal	2
3	2 random corners/1 per portal	2
4	2 random corners/2 per portal	4
5	2 random corners/1 per portal next higher tier	2
6	2 random corners/2 per portal next higher tier	4

Case Timeline Table	
Incident in Case Timeline	Caste of Dark Spawn Adversaries
Game 1	D6/D8
Game 2	D6/D8
Game 3	D6/D8
Game 4	D8/D10
Game 5	D8/D10
Game 6	D8/D10/Atrocity

Harvesting Arcana

Arcana is the generic term for a supernatural substance used by Hunters to upgrade their weapons, armor, Relics, and Satchels. Arcana can be harvested, or 'extracted', from any active Portal or Nexus by any player character. Portals may be harvested once per game. A Nexus may be harvested an unlimited number of times.

To extract Arcana, the Hunter must be in base-to-base contact with the scenic item or token and must roll a successful Interact Action. The character cannot use their Free Move for this Action, nor can they be prone or engaged in Melee Combat. The amount of Arcana extracted is always determined by the Hunter's Mind stat. It immediately goes into the Hunter's backpack to be disbursed for upgrades in-between missions (see Section 8, page 74).

Shutting Down a Nexus or Portals

A Nexus generates Portals. Portals generate Dark Spawn. Both can be shut down to reduce or remove Dark Spawn activity at the Incident site.

Portals

To close a Portal, a Hunter must roll a successful Interact Action while in base-to-base contact with the scenic item or token. It is important to note that Portals can only be shut down after the Nexus has materialized in the mission area – i.e. after three of the four Points of Interest have been cleared.

Once shut however, Dark Spawn can no longer enter via that corner. If Dark Spawn roll the number for a closed Portal at the start of a Dark Spawn phase, reroll for a new entry corner and abide by the result of the second roll. If you reroll a closed Portal, those Dark Spawn do not deploy that turn. Be aware a closed Portal cannot be harvested for Arcana.

Nexus Volatility

Closing a Nexus follows the same procedure – a successful Interact Action while in base-to-base contact with it. However, closing a Nexus requires three Interact Actions rather than one. These actions do not have to be performed by the same person nor accomplished within in the same turn.

Use glass stones or chits to mark successes and failures when attempting to close a Nexus. Three successes shut it down; three failures also close it, **but** summon a Terror-level enemy in its place. This D10 level adversary activates in the next Dark Spawn phase, along with any current or Portal-spawned enemies.

Like a Portal, a closed Nexus cannot be harvested for Arcana or searched for Clues; it must be active to be searched.

Ending the Incident

The Hunters can claim victory and end the mission when they have collected Clues from at least three of the four Points Of Interest and closed down the Nexus. Other than that, a game of *Nightmares* ends if all Nightwatch characters are either incapacitated or have fled; if the six-turn limit is reached before the objectives are fulfilled; or if the Hunters have voluntarily exited the mission area via any edge before the turn limit.

Any active but not out of action Hunters left on the board after the turn limit is reached must either make a Terror roll on the first turn of the next game at the start of the Dark Spawn Phase (they're traumatized after being left behind). Alternatively, they can roll on the Deep Scar and Odd Touch tables in Section 3 (page X), player's choice.

More Atmosphere

Incident not nightmarish enough for you? Feel like you and your crew are strolling through the park, kicking zombie puppies? Roll a D6 on the Creepy Conditions Table for a bit of extra tension.

Creepy Conditions Table	
D6 Roll	**Environment**
1	**Dark** – Minimal Line of Sight; Ranged Attacks are limited to 6".
2	**Gloomy** – You can see, sort of; Slightly better Line of Sight, Ranged Attacks are limited to 12".
3	**Flickering Lights** – Roll D6 at the start of each turn; on a 1–3 the turn is Dark, on a 4+ the turn is Well-lit.
4–6	**Well-Lit (or a Full Moon)** – You can see exactly what's coming at you; full range and Line of Sight.

Tactical Engagement Summary

1. All Tactical Engagements take place on a 2' x 2' mission area.
2. Battlefields are defined by four elements: Terrain, Points of Interest, Portals, and a Nexus.
3. *Nightmares* uses the IGO-UGO turn system with the Hunters activating first.
4. Tactical Engagements last six turns, or seven, if the crew gears up with melee and non-gunpowder ranged only.
5. The Hunters must gather Clues from three out of four POI and shut down the Nexus.
6. The Hunters deploy from the middle of the game area's edges. Dark Spawn models enter from the Portals at the corners.
7. Arcana can be extracted from active Portals and the Nexus. Portals can be harvested once, the Nexus unlimited times.
8. The Nexus will only materialize after three POI have been cleared.
9. Portals and the Nexus can be shut down by Interact Actions while a Hunter is base-to-base Interact actions. Portals require one successful Action. A Nexus requires three Actions.
10. Portals can be shut down but only after the Nexus has appeared.
11. Three failed attempts at closing a Nexus will close it, but immediately summons a Terror-level adversary in its place.
12. A Tactical Engagement ends when the turn limit is reached or when the Hunters have either accomplished the objectives, fled, or become incapacitated.

8 – A Full Case

Nightmares works for one-shot monster hunts. Gather your minis, make a crew, then start rolling dice and killing wretched gribblies. A good time at the game table.

However, *Nightmares* is really designed around the concept of a 'Full Case' – a series of six related Incidents that tell the story of how your team of occult vigilantes tracked down a dangerous supernatural threat. In the first five Incidents, players face ever more dangerous Dark Spawn minions. The final Incident is a confrontation with a final Boss – an Atrocity.

Generating a Full Case is a simple procedure, first select or roll the Inciting Incident on Table A (see Section 6, page 62), then roll and run each matched pair of Narrative Scenes and Tactical Engagements using the other Tables in that section. Without an official line of miniatures, game settings, and enemies are restricted only by the players' imaginations. The important elements to track in a Full Case are **Advances** for character improvement, **Upgrades** from collected Arcana, and **Favors** gained by disbursing leftover Clues.

The Rule of 666

Six is the magic number in *Nightmares*. Cases are made up of six Incidents. Character Advances require six Experience Points. Equipment Upgrades are purchased in increments of six Arcana. Favors, the last campaign detail, are purchased one-to-one with Clues.

Advances

Experience Points are tallied at the end of each Tactical Engagement and put into a common Crew Pool to be disbursed as best benefits the entire team (this cuts down on bookkeeping). One point is awarded for each of the following after every Incident:

- Leaving the mission area at the end of the game on your own two feet
- Killing at least one Dark Spawn adversary
- Clearing a Point Of Interest of Clues
- Closing a Portal or Nexus
- Healing or Reviving an Ally

Tally all Hunter accomplishments at the conclusion of the mission. Each increment of six Experience Points equals Advance. One Advance grants any one of the following benefits:

- Add 1 to any Narrative Scene die roll for a single Primal Attribute; the player must choose Body, Mind, or Spirit. This bonus is permanent for the remainder of the Case.
- Add 1" to character's base Move Rate.
- Grant one re-roll per Tactical Engagement for either Dodge Defend, Ranged Attack, or Melee Attack.

Upgrades

Improving Weapons and Gear is done with Arcana – the weird ectoplasmic goop recovered from Portals and Nexuses. Again, it is recommended all 'Arcana units' go into a general pool for common use.

- Increase a single weapon's Damage rating by 1 (up to a maximum of 3).
- Increase a Weaver's Relic Charge by 1.
- Increase a Wright's Satchel Capacity by 1.
- Purchase any two Esoterica Tokens.

Clues

When running a full Case, a crew must recover at least two Clues every Tactical Engagement to move onto the next Incident. Additional evidence recovered from Points of Interest becomes currency for Favors and extra Clues can be 'spent' to purchase Favors with the various NPC organizations. This is done on a one-to-one basis, one Clue for one Favor. Clues should be put in a common pool, but the specific recipient must be noted and assigned to an individual Hunter.

Common Items

Other than tracking Advances, Arcana, and Clues, *Nightmares* has no economy in the sense that players must "purchase" replacement Common Items (see Section 5, page 44). It's presumed that your dedicated crew of monster hunters ran to the pharmacy or the hardware store and got whatever was needed. Players simply load up before each Narrative Scene.

Likewise, Contraptions and Concoctions are replenished between games. The Wright's decision is simply what to pack. Relics recharge automatically between games and all spells are always available. The question the Weaver faces is what spell to cast at what strength?

But What If...

If hunting monsters were easy, then anyone could do it. Things never really go according to plan. In fact, sometimes, they go really, really bad. What happens if a Hunter dies or suffers a breakdown? Simply roll up new Hunter. They join the next Incident in the Case Timeline but have no commensurate experience. You've hired a new guy you found on the Dark Web. Good luck.

And if your crew gets hammered and has to bail without even getting two clues? Then re-fight the Tactical Engagement. The deployment consequences of the Narrative Scene stand, but maybe the fickle winds of fate will blow your way this time (this is meant to be fun, not punishment).

Optional Rule – Homeless Network

They're everywhere yet they go unnoticed. Once per Case, spending four Favors on the Homeless Network grants an automatic Success at any one Narrative Challenge – they know a thing, know a guy, know a way, provide a distraction, whatever is needed.

A Full Case Summary

1. Full Cases are six matched pairs of Narrative Scenes and Tactical Engagements.
2. Advances and Upgrades are purchased in increments of six.
3. Favors are purchased one-to-one for Clues. Favors are with specific NPC organizations and owed to specific player characters.
4. Common items are readily available. No purchase necessary.
5. Two Clues are needed to advance to the next Incident. Refight any battle you lose.
6. Help the Homeless and they'll help you.

9 – Last Words

Thank you for your interest in *When Nightmares Come*. Maybe it's just me, but Modern Horror feels a bit underserved in the miniatures wargame industry and I'm glad to offer this ruleset as a way to game out things like *Kolchak the Nightstalker*, *Supernatural*, *Black Summer*, *The Strain*, or even *X-Files*, *Shaun the Dead*, and *Scooby-Doo* (but with guns). I hope you enjoy it. At the very least, it's a good excuse to get together with friends, get cool minis on the table, forge a narrative, and start killing monsters.

Special thanks to Cape Cod Wargame Commission, the Majestic Gamers in Corvallis, Oregon, and the excellent bunch at the Stalker7 Facebook Group. You have my eternal gratitude.

Good hunting.

Patrick Todoroff
Stalker7.com

Quick Reference Sheet

Turn Sequence
Hunters' Activations
- Hunters always go first. Players Activate their hunters, one at a time, completing all actions before moving to the next. The order is determined by the players, if this cannot be agreed then roll off.

Dark Spawn Activations
- After the Hunters have all Activated, then the Dark Spawn.

Actions
- Action Dice Pool: D10, D8, D6. Each Die may only be used once, in any order.
- Free Move: Hunters have a free move. Move up to full value of Move Rate. May be replaced by certain Use actions.

Action List
- **Aim – (Melee or Ranged):** +1 attacker's roll and -2 defenders Dodge Defend roll.
- **Attack (Melee):** 1 attack in melee combat.
- **Attack (Ranged):** 1 attack in ranged combat.
- **Concentrate Fire:** Allows multiple hunters to target, see page 22.
- **Dodge Defend:** used to save against attacks. Armor roll + cover/equipment. Dark Spawn use Quality Die. Atrocities use Armor.
- **Interact:** Non-combat interaction with terrain or other models.
- **Move:** Model moves up to its Move Rate. Affected by Terrain.
- **Overwatch:** Hunters and Atrocities only. Set aside two action dice to perform one action in an enemy's activation.
- **Reload:** Single-shot weapons only. May be used instead of free move. Otherwise requires a Use action.
- **Special/Skill Check:** Complex tasks relating to mission or narrative objectives
- **Throw Grenade/Weapon:** Make a ranged attack using a thrown weapon (see page 28)
- **Use:** Non-combat personal actions/using a model's equipment.

Movement
- **Climbing:** Ladders/stairs full Move Rate. Otherwise climbing is at half Move Rate, no other actions other than Move may be performed while climbing.
- **Obstacles:** 1" extra movement per Obstacle.
- **Jumping:** 1" gaps require 1" extra movement. Gaps over 1" may not be jumped.
- **Difficult Terrain:** move at half Move Rate.

Combat
Melee Attacks Sequence
- Select one Die Type from Action Dice Pool.
- Select target
- Roll dice, success on a 4+ (+/- modifiers). TDB if applicable.
- If successful, then the defender makes their Dodge Defend roll, 4+ (+/- modifiers).
- Multiple Attacks can be made in a single activation, so long as the activated model has Action Dice remaining in their Action Dice Pool.
- Dark Spawn use their relevant caste-level dice.
- **Locked in Melee:** If a model is still in melee combat next turn, must engage in melee or attempt to disengage (see page 27).
- **Multiple Combats:** Split combats in 1-on-1s if possible. A model attacked by multiple enemies suffers -1 Penalty to their Dodge Defend roll for every attacker after the first.

Ranged Attacks
- Select one Die Type from Action Dice Pool.
- Select target, make sure it is in Range and Line of Sight.
- Roll dice, success on a 4+ (+/- modifiers). TDB if applicable.
- If successful, then the defender makes their Dodge Defend roll, 4+ (+/- modifiers).

Indirect Ranged Attacks
- Follows steps for Ranged Attacks with the following alterations:
- Does not need LoS, but does need to be in range.
- -1 if can see target, -3 if cannot.
- If roll successful, on target. If not, then drifts (see page 30)

Terrain Modifiers

- **Obstruction:** items that obscure but do not block LoS. -1 to Attack Roll. Cumulative with other Obstructions, Concealment, and Cover.
- **Concealment:** things hide rather .than protect -2 to Attack Roll.
- **Cover:** Things that protect.-2 to Attack Roll and + 2 to Dodge Defend Roll.
- **Elevated:** reduce defender's terrain modifier by 1 step (see page 26)

Wounds

- No wounds = All die types, Free Move and three Actions
- 1 wound = no D10. May take Free Move and two Actions at D8 and D6.
- 2 wounds = no D10 or D8. May take Free Move and one Action at D6
- 3 wounds = Free Move only.
- 4 wounds = The Hunter is **dead.** May be revived.

Terror and Dread

- Terror: The first time a Hunter's model comes within 6" and line-of-sight of a Dark Spawn model with the 'Repulsive' Trait. Immediately roll their full Action Dice Pool (4+ successes required). Any fails are removed from their Action Dice Pool next Activation. The following turn the Action Dice Pool resets.

- Dread: Hunters must make a Dread roll if they suffer a number of Hits equal to or exceeding their Resolve in a single turn. Roll D6 and consult Dread Table, page 31.

Narrative Scene Summary

1. Narrative Scenes are defined by four questions: What? Where? Who? When? Roll on Tables A, B, C, and D for specifics (see pages 62 and 64)
2. The number of Challenges in a Narrative Scene is equal to the number of NPC Organizations. Challenges are non-combat obstacles the Hunters must address to gain access to the Incident site.
3. Narrative Scene Challenges refer to the Hunters' Primal Attributes and are resolved by rolling the appropriate die type.
4. Narrative Scene Challenges are solved by one of three methods: Physical, Reason, Charm.
5. Players discuss and select whichever method they want when facing a Challenge, but each method can only be used once per Narrative Scene.
6. The details of a Narrative Scene's Challenges are made up by the players and are decided collectively, using Group Rolls of appropriate die type.
7. Connections and Favors can be used once per Narrative Scene to turn the results of any one failed die roll into a success. Connections are never spent. Favors are single-use but can be purchased with Clues.

Character Sheet

Character Name:			

Character Class:	Primary Fighting Method:		
Primal Attribute	Body:	Mind:	Spirit:
Move Rate			
Equipment Slots			
Extraction Efficiency			
Resolve			
Relic Charge/Satchel Capacity			

Action Die Pool

Two Dice Bonus

General Ability

Class Skill

Connections

Favors

Weapons and Equipment					
Weapon	Heft	Uses/Turn	Range	Rate of Fire	Damage
Equipment Slots					

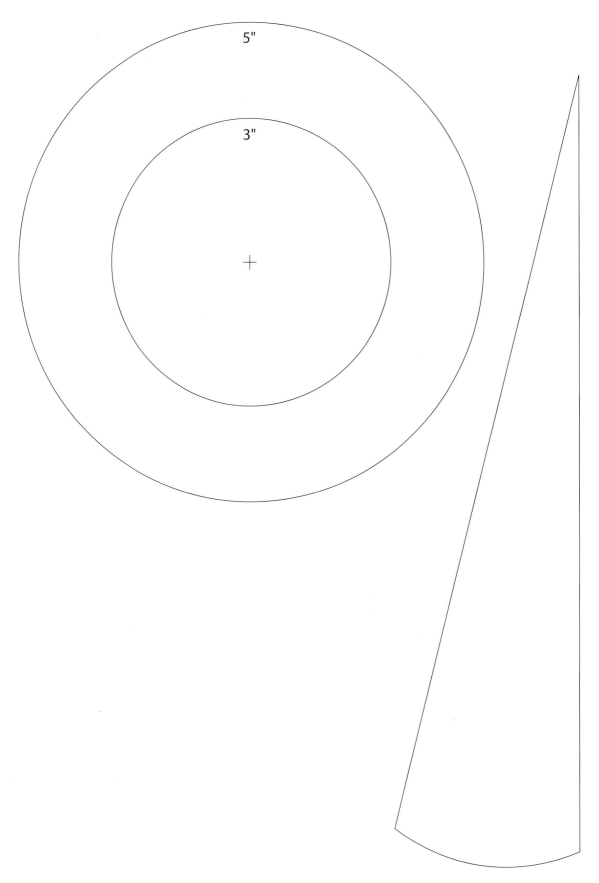

5"

3"